SAFE AT HOME

Also by Alison Gordon

Fiction

The Dead Pull Hitter *1988*

Non-Fiction

Foul Balls: Five Years in
the American League *1984*

5P

SAFE AT HOME

A KATE HENRY MYSTERY

m - GO
1990

A novel by

Alison Gordon

St. Martin's Press
New York

/

Library of Congress Cataloging-in-Publication Data

Gordon, Alison.
    Safe at home / Alison Gordon.
        p.   cm.
    ISBN 0-312-05959-0
    I. Title.
PR9199.3.G617S24   1991
813'.54—dc20   90-29134
                                                                CIP

First published in Canada by McClelland & Stewart Inc.

10 9 8 7 6 5 4 3 2

For Paul – without your impatience,
I could never have written this.

ACKNOWLEDGEMENTS

Heartfelt thanks to those who encouraged and helped me with this book: The Ontario Arts Council, Lee Davis Creal, Ellen Seligman, James Polk, Mary Adachi, Hidemi Kihira, Charles Gordon, Ruth Gordon, Sara Murdoch, Staff Sergeant Bob Adair, Andy Moir, and Henri Fiks (the Wizard of DOS).

SAFE AT HOME

CHAPTER

1

The sexual tension in the air was so thick you could cut it with a knife. Unfortunately, all I had was a pair of chopsticks.

I reached out with my right foot and found Andy's underneath the table. He wiggled his toes in his socks, stroking the arch of my foot while he chatted in Japanese with the kimono-clad waitress. It was almost unbearably erotic.

When the waitress left the private tatami room, sliding the rice-paper door shut behind her, he smiled, a little too smugly, I thought.

"What's the news from the south?" he asked. "Are the Titans going to the World Series this year?"

The bastard. I'd been away for almost two months. The one weekend he was supposed to come to Florida, he'd had to work. We were together again, and he wanted to talk sports? He doesn't even like baseball.

"That's what the wise guys say," I said, playing his game. "I think they've been listening to Fric and Frac too much."

Fric and Frac, or Ted Ferguson and Red O'Brien to their mothers, are the owner and manager, respectively, of the Toronto Titans baseball team, the happy band of overgrown adolescents with whom I spend my days between February and October. As the chief baseball writer for the Toronto *Planet*, I cover most of the home games and do the bulk of the travelling with the team.

Hence my long absence. Spring training, not half as glamorous as it sounds, had me roving around Arizona and Florida for nearly six weeks. The season began on the road, so I spent another ten days in Seattle, Oakland, and Anaheim sending back dispatches of disaster to the home fans.

"Seven straight losses isn't much of a way to start a season, is it?"

Andy thoughtfully nibbled some grilled eel and ran his foot slowly up my calf.

"With a rainout thrown in for good measure," I said, spreading my legs.

When his foot found the path, I slammed my knees shut, trapping him. Then I tickled. For a tough guy, he's easy to render helpless. Luckily, this vulnerability hasn't yet become widely known in criminal circles.

Andy, by the way, is a cop. The best staff sergeant on the homicide squad, as a matter of fact, and if you think that a lady sportswriter and a police officer make for a pretty peculiar romantic pairing, you're not alone.

2

We met last fall. It wasn't a traditional introduction, by any means. We met over a small matter of murder, two murders to be precise. The victims were Sultan Sanchez and Steve Thorson, a designated hitter and star pitcher for the Titans. Someone had used their skulls for batting practice.

While Andy was looking for the killer, I was looking for a scoop. I got it when I almost became the third victim.

Andy rode to the rescue in the final reel of that movie, and we've been together, sort of, ever since. The relationship is complicated by the fact that we both have strange working hours, healthy egos, and a certain wariness about entanglements. Andy is divorced, the father of two boys. I was just getting over a six-year-long relationship, after the man I lived with realized that I liked the road and didn't want to have his babies. I thought it was women who were supposed to listen to biological clocks ticking. If I have one, it runs on batteries, silently.

Andy orchestrated my homecoming. I had hoped he would meet me at the airport with an armload of flowers, followed by an afternoon spent sipping champagne in bed, the one place we always get along. Instead I'd humped my own bags through Terminal One, stood in line for a cab for half an hour, and was greeted at home only by Elwy, my fat black-and-white cat, who sulked in a closet to show his disapproval of my long absence. Andy was just a message on my answering machine telling me he was sorry that he was too busy to meet me, but that he'd be by at 7:00. I spent the afternoon doing laundry and feeling sorry for myself.

He arrived late, with flowers and Dom Perignon – "for later," he said. I had martini glasses chilling in the freezer and satin sheets on the bed, but he rushed me out the door without a word of consultation. Cops are like that. Hell, *men* are like that.

I stopped being annoyed when I saw what he had done. He took me to Kuri, the restaurant where we'd had our first date, if a discussion of murder can be so described. We've been there often since, and the owner watches over our relationship as if it had been his idea in the first place.

He and Andy are particularly close. Andy spent several years teaching English at a Japanese university and has an enduring love for the country. He keeps his Japanese in shape talking with Kuri, who is very patient with him.

The two of them had devised a welcoming feast of many courses. By the third flask of sake, I'd decided that Andy was a romantic genius. I was even glad we hadn't leapt right into bed. I had forgotten how aphrodisiac anticipation can be.

The door slid open again. This time it was Kuri himself, with more sake.

"Everything is all right?"

"Perfect, Kuri-san," I said. "Please join us."

"Just for one minute," he said.

As well as being a mother hen to Andy and me, Kuri is a baseball fanatic, having transferred his allegiance from the Japanese Hanshin Tigers to the Titans, so the minute stretched into fifteen while the next course was served. He was anxious for news of Atsuo Watanabe, the Japanese player the Titans had brought over for a look-see in spring training. He'd done well enough to grab the shortstop job with the

Triple A team, and Kuri wanted to know all about it.

I had lots to tell him. The cultural clashes and misunderstandings between Watanabe and the Americans and players from the Dominican Republic had made for an interesting spring camp. He worked harder than any other two players combined, and his elaborate respect for the manager and coaches was unlike anything I had seen before. The other Titans were appalled, but I figured they could learn a thing or two from him.

Kuri was also worried, as was I, about the fate of his favourite Titan player, Tiny Washington, the wonderful first baseman who had been in a slump since spring training began. With a player in the minors waiting to take his place, his future looked gloomy. The kid was ready: he'd been an International League All-Star for two seasons. It made perfect baseball sense. But that didn't mean it didn't bother Tiny or his fans.

Andy, while smiling politely, was obviously fed up with the jock talk by the time Kuri bowed his way back to work.

"Don't look at me that way," I said. "It was your idea to come here. Besides, you brought up the subject."

"But I exhausted my knowledge in the first thirty seconds," he laughed.

"All right, then. Tell me what you're working on."

"The same thing I've been on since just after you left," he sighed. "Those two murders of children."

"Two?"

"I told you about them on the phone. The first was a ten-year-old boy."

"I remember. He was drugged and raped."

"There was another one a few weeks later. A twelve-year-old this time."

"And you think it's the same guy?"

"Yes. We suspected it right from the start because of the similarities between the two crimes. Once the forensics came back it was clear that they were killed by the same man."

"Is there a connection between the two kids?"

"Not an obvious one. The first one lived and went to school in Forest Hill. The second one was from Regent Park."

No, the paths of a child of privilege and a child of poverty were unlikely to cross.

"We're going through all the routine stuff: interviewing neighbours where the kids lived and where the bodies were found, checking parking tickets, bringing in the kiddy diddlers."

"The what?"

"Child molesters. Sorry."

I wasn't offended. Cops talk less crudely than most journalists.

"We put all the data we could gather in one of the new super-duper computers and have come up with nothing. Zip. A big fat zero."

"Are you under a lot of pressure on this one?"

"Where shall I start? With the chief? He's on the phone a couple of times a day. With the press? The papers are calling the murderer the Daylight Stalker. Your paper has assigned two reporters full-time to the case. They've interviewed everybody even remotely connected with the deaths and they won't leave me alone."

"Who are they?"

"The regular police-beat guy, Jimmy Peterson. He's not so bad. He understands how we work. The other one's some broad named Margaret Papadakis. She's a real pain in the ass."

I smiled. She would be. A smart, tough, tenacious, and very ambitious junior reporter who realizes that this kind of story can make a career. She knows how to ring the changes of tragedy, and stay on page one with it.

"She's just doing her job, Andy." He grunted and poured more sake in both our cups. "You're not going to sucker me into an argument tonight, Kate. Or else I'll forget why I missed you so much."

He leaned over and got his coat, which was lying a few feet away. He took a small box out of the pocket.

"Sorry it's not wrapped," he said.

Touched, I fumbled with the box. For one irrational moment I was afraid it was going to be a ring. Instead, it was a stunning pair of earrings in silver and onyx. They were very simple, in the shape of a stylized fan: modern, but with a touch of deco in the design.

"If you don't like them, I can exchange them."

"They're perfect," I said. I took off the earrings I was wearing and put on the new ones, then pulled my unruly red hair back and up to show them off.

"Beautiful," he said, then slid around to my side of the table.

"Can we go home now?" I asked in a few minutes.

"If we don't we're going to get Kuri in trouble with the morality squad," he said.

We went from the restaurant to my house. There is no my-place-or-yours choice in our relationship. I've spent a night or two with him at his fairly spartan apartment, but my house is cosier and better equipped. We've never talked about living together, but he has gradually made his presence felt: a toothbrush and razor in my medicine cabinet, a couple of clean shirts in my closet, that sort of thing. He has brought over books he's reading, some music he particularly likes. During the winter we spent a lot of domestic evenings and Sunday afternoons in front of the fire.

He has a key, which is an admission on my part that he's the only man in my life. But I don't think we are likely to make a move in the immediate future, and not just because he needs his own place when he has his kids for the weekend. He likes to retreat, and I'm usually grateful when he does.

Not the night I got home, though. We were both advancing as soon as we got in the door.

We broke apart long enough to take off our coats. He hung his up, then his jacket. Finally he unstrapped his shoulder holster and put his gun carefully on the shelf in its usual place behind some hats I'd bought in a weak moment.

"Aw, gee, and I thought you were just glad to see me," I said. Old joke.

"I'll get the champagne, then I'll show you just how glad I am," he said, leering like Groucho Marx.

I was putting some sultry jazz on the machine when there was a knock on the door.

It was my downstairs tenant, cat-sitter, and friend Sally Parkes, in an outrageous kimono, Elwy in her arms.

"Hey, Katie, good to see you," she said. She is the only person I allow to use that name. "I wasn't sure you were back yet. Elwy came down for a bit of attention, but I thought I'd better return him."

"He's not speaking to me, but thanks anyway," I said, plopping him down on the couch and giving her a hug. "How have you been? And what have you done to your hair?"

Her blonde curls had given way to modified spikes feathering all over her head.

"You've got to look the part on Queen Street West," she said. "Besides, I was sick of being mistaken for Shirley Temple."

Sally works at a photo gallery in Toronto's avant-garde district, surrounded by punks, prostitutes, and performance artists – black leather for days. It's quite a change for a woman from a small

Saskatchewan town who was once married to a New Democratic Party Member of Parliament. Her husband lost his seat in the house and his confidence, and left her for an earnest young socialist with big boobs and a thing for older men.

Sally and I were friends at the University of Saskatchewan, but we had lost touch over the years. We met again at a ballet class a couple of years ago when she was left adrift with her son, T.C. I was looking for a tenant after my former lasting relationship didn't, and both problems got solved at once.

"Well, you'd never be let on the Good Ship Lollipop looking like that," I said. "It looks, well, fine. Different, but good."

"Thanks for your enthusiastic support," she said. "If you had really liked it, I would have worried."

The champagne cork popped in the kitchen.

"Oh, sorry. I thought you were alone."

"Don't worry about it."

Andy came into the room.

"Hi Sally," he said, warmly. "I'll get another glass."

One of the many nice things about Andy is that he doesn't resent my friends. One of the few nice things about me is that I don't automatically drop my women friends when a new man appears on the scene, and I think he appreciates that. In fact, he's become part of the family, and seems to be as happy to know Sally and her son T.C. as he is to know me.

Nonetheless, I was glad when Sally, no dummy, declined his offer and went downstairs to bed.

Andy and I settled in on one of the couches, his arms around me. It felt wonderful.

"Is it true? Am I really not in a hotel? I'm really home," I sighed. "Do you want me to light a fire?"

"You already have," he said, and kissed me.

The phone rang. We both groaned.

"Let's not answer it," I said.

"Sorry, you have to."

Andy's semi-residence at my house means that my number is on file at the homicide squad. An apologetic desk sergeant was on the line. I passed Andy the phone.

"Yeah, Munro," he grumbled. "This had better be important."

I tried to figure out what was going on by Andy's reactions. It didn't sound good. He grimaced at me.

"All right," he finally said. "Tell Jim I'll meet him there. Put MacPherson on."

He covered the mouthpiece.

"Kate, I'm really sorry," he said, and looked it. "Another little boy has been murdered."

He took my hand, then went back to the phone. Damn, damn, shit, piss.

"Yeah, Don, I'm at Kate Henry's," he said. "Come pick me up. You remember the address?"

I tugged at his hand.

"Tell him to take the long way," I whispered. He smiled and shook his head.

"I'll be downstairs in five minutes," he said.

I yanked my hand out of his as he hung up the phone, got up and went to the closet.

"Kate, I'm sorry."

"One night, God," I said, raising my eyes to the ceiling. "Is that asking for too much? One lousy night without the phone ringing? What did I do to deserve this?"

11

I pulled his coat and jacket out of the closet and threw them at him. He caught them, then walked past me to get his gun.

"I know I'm being selfish," I said. "But it's been two months since I've seen you. It's been two months since we've made love. Aren't I even allowed to get pissed off?"

"Maybe I can get back later."

"Don't bother."

"For God's sake, Kate. Stop it!" he snapped. "Some things are just a bit more important than our sex life."

"Just because you're right doesn't mean I have to like it," I said. "Or that I can cope with it. We can't live this way. I can't just turn off and on depending on the little bits of time you can fit into your crime-fighting schedule."

"Don't, Kate, please," he said, putting his arms around me and drawing me close. I kept my hands at my sides and turned my head away from his mouth.

"This isn't going to work," I said.

He sighed, let me go, and turned for the door.

"I hope you're wrong," he said, "but I haven't got time to discuss it now. I'll call you when I can."

He shut the door quietly behind him, and I listened to his footsteps going down the stairs. I lit a cigarette and went to the front window. He was pacing on the sidewalk in front of the house. I almost went down to him to make it up, but his ride arrived before I could. As the car pulled away, his face turned towards my window.

I was suddenly very tired. I put the champagne back into the fridge with a silver spoon, handle down, in the mouth of the bottle. That's supposed to keep the bubbles. I'd never had enough left in a bottle to test the theory before.

I washed the glasses, turned out the lights and got my comforting blue flannel nightie out of the bottom drawer. Satin sheets are cold to sleep in alone.

Before I turned out the light, I whistled for Elwy. He came to the door, looked at me, and padded pointedly away.

Welcome home, Kate.

CHAPTER

3

It was almost dawn when Andy came back. I didn't hear him. He was just suddenly there, with his arms around me and his whiskers scratching my neck. We had a spectacular reconciliation. I fell asleep again with tears on my cheeks. Not all of them were mine.

When I woke up a few hours later, I found myself among friends. Elwy was on one side of me, purring in his sleep. Andy was on the other, snoring. I extricated myself gently, found my nightie, and went to the kitchen. It was still early, but I felt too cheerful to waste the morning in bed.

I put on the kettle and went down for the papers. There was nothing about the latest murder, which had been discovered after the morning edition deadline, but the 7:00 CBC Radio news led with it.

The victim was an eleven-year-old Chinese boy. His nude body had been found in an empty warehouse. Like the first two victims, he had been raped.

A police spokesman – Andy, presumably – had not ruled out any connection with the murders of the two other children.

Elwy, who can hear the tiniest of kitchen sounds from the deepest sleep, was butting my ankles and demanding food before the tea had steeped, but Andy didn't stir until I'd finished my second cup. When I heard him in the shower, I started his coffee.

By the time he emerged, wrapped in a towel, looking damp, groggy, and sexy, I had his cup poured, complete with a revolting three sugars. He mumbled his thanks, directed a kiss somewhere in the vicinity of my right ear and took the paper to the kitchen table.

"Breakfast?" We're seldom temperamentally compatible in the mornings. Because I was one hour and two cups of tea up on him, I was the brighter, for a change.

"Maybe in a minute," he said, blowing on his coffee to cool it enough to drink.

There was no point trying for conversation. I took my good spirits into the shower. When I got out, Andy was up to speed.

"Did you leave any hot water for me to shave?"

"About as much as you left me to shower," I said. "Wait twenty minutes and it will be fine."

"I haven't got twenty minutes," he said, wiping steam from the mirror. "You should have woken me earlier."

"Not my job, chief."

I went and poured another cup of tea, my own blend of Irish Breakfast and Earl Grey, ambrosia after the tea-bag slop from metal pots I'd been suffering in American hotels. I took it back and perched on the edge of the tub to watch him shave.

"Another little boy, eh? Is it the same guy?"

"It looks like it," he said, through the lather, then paused and looked at me in the mirror.

"Normal rules, right?"

"Of course."

One way we've been able to get along as a couple has been to keep our conversations off the record. Andy, as most of us, needs a sounding board. He wouldn't usually choose a reporter for that role, but I feel no need to share his conversations with colleagues. When we met, the Titan murders were on my beat, and we stepped all over each other in our investigations, but I don't normally cover crime. This is not to say that my colleagues who do haven't tried to get information from me, but I have no conflict in loyalties. Besides, I love the inside stuff so much that I'd be crazy to jeopardize my source, and I like to think that my contributions are useful. As I often remind him, I found the Titan killer before he did. He doesn't like the reminders much, but still talks to me.

"We might have a break with this one. There were some signs of struggling. We hope he might have some tissue under his fingernails to link him to the killer."

"And the guy might have scratches."

"Right. The other two were drugged, and there was no sign of a struggle with either one. Forensics found a mild sedative, like valium, in the stomach contents. That hardly narrows down the field of suspects."

"So, what do you think? He slips them a mickey, molests them, then kills them to shut them up?"

"No. The first boy. Benjamin Goldman, was killed first, then raped. The second, Marc LeBlanc, was raped first. So was this one, with a bit more violence, it looks like. He's getting more confident."

"Oh, God."

"They've all been killed by suffocating, probably with a dry-cleaning bag. We're pretty sure it's the same guy now, but we can't find the connection."

"Maybe there isn't one. Maybe it's just random."

"If it is, we're going to have an even harder time finding him. We'll just keep looking for the link."

"What do you know about the kids? Don't their parents keep track of them? How could they just disappear?"

"They were good kids. They'd never been in trouble. There was no reason not to trust them on their own. The one last night was on his way to school from swimming practice. His teachers figured he was home sick."

"I can't stop thinking about their parents."

"Neither can I. My own boys take the subway when they come to see me. Why not? I've never given it any thought. They're responsible kids. But next time I'll pick them up."

He rinsed his face and towelled it dry, then stared at himself in the mirror. His eyes caught mine in the glass.

"I'm going to get this son-of-a-bitch, Kate. I promise you that."

He went into the bedroom. I followed him and did my best to deter him from dressing, with little success. I had to be losing my touch. Or maybe it was the flannel nightie.

"Okay, get off me," he laughed. "What's your day like?"

"It's going to be crazy," I said. "Opening day is wild enough, but this one is going to be doubly insane in the new stadium."

The equivalent of the gross national product of an emerging nation had been spent by several levels of government and a consortium of corporations to build a palace of pleasure with a retractable roof, all part of Toronto's obsession with being "world class." I hadn't seen it since it had been finished, but by all reports, it was spectacular.

"Will the roof work?"

"They say it will. I still have to be convinced. Right now I'm more worried about the press box, and about finding my way around."

"Where's your sense of occasion?"

"When the occasion is opening day, all I can think about is the drunks in the stands and the streakers on the field. I'll start enjoying it tomorrow, when the place isn't filled with event freaks."

"Just a typical cynical sportswriter," he teased.

"On the contrary, a romantic who doesn't want strangers sullying the purity of my game."

"When will you be done?"

"About eight, I would think."

"I probably won't be, but I'll call you later."

At the door, he hugged me hard.

"I'm glad I came back last night," he said.

"So am I. Be careful out there, all right?"

"You watch too much television."

CHAPTER

4

Despite my protests to Andy, I was kind of excited about opening day in the new stadium. I left for work before I had to, because I was itchy to get going. Besides, I wanted to drive my car for the first time in two months.

I traded my aging sportscar in on a reconditioned Citroën Deux Chevaux when the snows came last fall. With its snail-shaped body and peculiar gear-shift, it looks more like a toy than a car. I've had people pat it when I'm stopped at crosswalk.

It coughed a bit, the way I do on a bad morning, before the engine caught. I kept the rag top closed. It was mild for Toronto in April, but my blood had thinned in Florida.

I had decided to pay a rare visit to the office on the way to the ballpark. I hadn't seen the boys in a while, and my mailbox could probably stand emptying. Besides, Jake Watson, my editor, likes to see me in the flesh from time to time to make sure there isn't an imposter cashing my cheques.

I don't spend much time at the paper because most of my work is done at the ballpark or at home, thanks to my handy-dandy micro-computer and modem, but that suits me fine. The *Planet* offices always depress me. At the risk of sounding like a terrible old fart, newspapers aren't what they used to be.

It's the quiet that bothers me. There's no shouting for copy boys (there are no copy boys, even, just office persons), no typewriters clattering or phones ringing; just the eerie clicking of computer keys and the muted warbling of the phones I still don't know how to use. Besides, they won't let me smoke any more.

It was just 10:30 when I arrived. The toy department, as some call our corner of the world, was pretty empty, but the coffee wagon which makes its daily stop right next to my desk had drawn a crowd.

This meant that catching up on all the office gossip was easy. There was also the usual advice tendered about how the Titans could turn things around. And I wasn't at all surprised when the beautiful and ambitious Margaret Papadakis parked her shapely butt on the corner of my desk.

"Andy Munro's a pretty tough case," she tried, for openers.

"He sure is," I smiled.

"Have you talked to him since the latest murder?"

"We've had words," I said.

"Did he tell you about it? It was pretty gruesome."

"The old faithful 'grisly discovery,' eh? What would you police reporters do without that phrase?"

"Come on, Kate. Whose side are you on?"

"In this instance, I don't believe I'm on anyone's side, Margaret. I didn't know there were sides."

I felt slightly torn, in fact. The journalist in me identified with Margaret. Cops, including Andy, as I well know from frustrating experience, don't trust reporters, and the sensationalist coverage we give crimes like these doesn't help the situation.

Sometimes, obviously, it is in their interest to get publicity. The problem for reporters like Margaret is that when they do decide it is in their interest to let go of some information, they do it in convoluted policespeak. Try making lively copy out of doubletalk about "alleged perpetrators" and "probable assailants" when your readers are screaming for the blood of the Daylight Stalker.

On the other hand, hard work overcomes all sorts of adversity. I had ended up getting the story myself. If a lowly sports reporter, looked down upon by hotshots like her, had done it, why couldn't she?

"Sorry, Margaret. I'd like to help you, but I've got a conflict. I'm sure you understand."

She reached across my desk and dropped her empty coffee cup in my wastepaper basket. Then she smiled and stood up, smoothing her snug leather skirt over her hips.

"I guess I'll have to see if I can develop some sources of my own," she said, before gliding across the room.

Bitch. Worse, a gorgeous bitch under thirty who was on a story with my man. I felt like a character out of the afternoon soaps the ballplayers like so much. I'd have to ask one of them how Pamela or Tiffany would handle the situation.

I put my nasty thoughts aside and began going through a six-inch stack of press releases and mail from readers. Mine is the worst desk in the office. We each have to share a large work station, as they are now called, with another reporter, with only a foot-high partition between us. Because I'm so seldom there, they figured it was a good dumping spot for Richard Greaves, the school sports guy. He's an eager little beaver who doesn't realize that the only reason his stories get into the paper is so that kids and their parents can see their names in print. But Dickie takes his job more seriously than the publisher does.

You can't fault his dedication. He bombs around in an old van with his camera equipment in the back, covering the games he thinks are most important. He's not a bad photographer, either, and he can put together a good little round-up with all the names spelled right. He's also got a good network of young stringers who phone him in the scores.

It's a thankless job, but he does it really well. Not that anyone else notices. Because he hasn't got a major beat, the poor guy is dumped on a lot by the other reporters, so I usually try to be nice to him. Besides, he's good-looking and quite charming. If only he would shut up occasionally.

"Have you heard about my tournament, Kate?"

"Can't say that I have."

"I'm trying to get the *Planet* to sponsor a kids' baseball tournament this summer. What do you think?"

"Aren't there already dozens of little league tournaments?"

"Not like this one. We would have big prizes and lots of publicity. It would be good for the paper."

And for Dickie, I suppose. He was doing a bit of empire-building. If he couldn't get the major beat he lusted after, he was going to turn his little corner of the section into something important.

"It's not a bad idea," I said.

"I'd like to get the Titans involved," he said. "I was thinking maybe some of the players could give out the prizes, or maybe they could supply free tickets to Titan games. What do you think?"

"They might go for it," I said.

"Let's have a beer later and talk about it," he said, putting on the charm. "I'd like to tell you my ideas. Maybe you can put in a word to Jake. Besides, I want to hear all about Florida."

Promises don't cost anything. I said I'd see him later. Much later, I promised myself. Appeased, he went back to his interminable phone calls.

After a few minutes, Jake Watson stopped by my desk on his way back from the morning editorial meeting. It was good to see him, fat and sweating in his ubiquitous winter tweed suit. He was one of those WASP Canadians with British pretensions, the black sheep of his banking family. When the season changed, he would be in seersucker. I could hardly wait. The tweed was starting to take on a life of its own.

"Hi, stranger," he said. "Good to have you back. Care to step into my office?"

"Yes, sir, boss, sir," I said. Jake was a friend, and nothing annoyed him more than when I kowtowed.

This time he just laughed as he put an arm across my shoulder and escorted me to his office.

He closed the door behind us and pulled an ashtray out of his bottom desk drawer. We lit up like naughty children behind the barn.

"You've got to say one thing about those juiceless bastards and their bylaws," he said, exhaling with pleasure. "They've put the adventure back in smoking."

"Yeah, sure. You've got an office door to close."

"Doesn't mean there haven't been complaints. Hell, let them fire me. I'd retire to the Dominican Republic on my severance pay. Speaking of which tropical paradise, how is the pride of San Pedro looking?"

He was referring to Alejandro Jones, the blithe spirit who plays second base for the Titans, last season's American League rookie of the year and one-man proof that baseball can still be fun in the era of big paydays and crushing performance pressure.

"He's fine. If anyone can get them out of this tailspin, it's Alex. If only the rest of them were like him."

"What about the losing streak? Should you be putting that in any sort of context?"

"Lots of teams have lost seven straight to start the season. They've got a long way to go before they threaten the record. Talk to me in a week, maybe, but right now, I don't see any reason to cover them in anything but a normal way."

"Feel the same way about Washington's slump?"

"That's different. I wouldn't be surprised to see them bring up Kid Cooper. He's ready, and when you're going this bad at Tiny's age, it might be something more than a slump. I don't think they're going to give him a chance to work out of it."

"Want to write about it?"

"Let's wait until something happens. I know what I want to say, and I've put together some stuff on his career, ready to go. I don't want to run it yet, though."

"We can't be sure the other papers won't jump the gun."

"No, we can't but I don't want to be a ghoul. I'm not going to count Tiny out until he's been benched."

Jake looked sceptical.

"We're not talking about a major scoop here, Jake. Let them write his epitaph before he's cold, if they want. You know mine's going to be better, whenever it comes out."

"Handy having you back in town, Kate," Jake smiled. "Else I might not remember how indispensable you are."

"If you'd ever compliment me, I wouldn't have to congratulate myself all the time," I said.

"Not my style. Anything else going on I should know about?"

"Something's up with Joe Kelsey. I can't figure out what it is, but he's gone inside himself, somehow. He's never been exactly gregarious, but these days he's really withdrawn."

"It doesn't seem to be affecting him on the field."

"Oh, he's playing better than ever. He just doesn't seem to be enjoying it as much. Anyway, it's not a story. Just a little mystery. And he's avoiding me like mad."

Joe Kelsey, also known as Preacher, is the left fielder. He's an earnest black man from Oakland who has been in the Titan organization since he left high school. He went a bit wild for a year in the minor leagues, getting mixed up with drugs and, apparently, some sexual experimentation he'd like to forget, but found God, cleaned up his act, and has been solid ever since. He doesn't thump the Bible excessively, which is fine with me.

He's a complicated guy, always has been, but before this season has always talked freely to me.

"You'll figure it out, eventually," Jake said. "When are you going to the ballpark?"

"Soon. I've got to explore. Besides, I want to beat the traffic."

"I've got a parking pass for you here somewhere. And your Titan credentials."

"Thanks. Who else have you got covering?"

"Jeff's doing a column. I'm sending Roger Chan, the new kid, to do a sidebar. Tell him what you want. Cityside is sending three or four bodies to cover the stadium, the traffic, and the fans. You and Jeff figure out how to divide up the rest. I'll probably come down myself for a couple of innings. Bill Spencer and Jay Morse are the photographers. Let them know if you want anything special."

"Well, I might ask them to get some candid stuff of Tiny, just in case."

"Thanks."

"Oh, by the way, I've got two months' worth of expense sheets for you to sign."

"The only thing you can be counted on to hand in on time. Get out of here."

"Yes, boss."

CHAPTER

5

Jeff Glebe bummed a ride to the ballpark with me, which is always an adventure. First there's the problem of fitting his six-foot five-inch frame into my tiny car. The two of us with our briefcases and equipment make for a snug fit. I opened the roof so we could have the illusion of being able to breathe.

The second problem is that Jeff is an extremely nervous passenger. He never says much, but his grip on the door handle and audible intakes of breath are clue enough. And I'm a good driver.

"Relax, Stretch, I'm not going to kill either one of us," I laughed, glancing over at him, which made him whimper.

We were on the Gardiner Expressway going west, with eighteen-wheelers roaring by in the passing lane. I was going more slowly than usual in deference to Jeff's sensitive psyche, but it didn't seem to help.

"Why did I come with her? I forgot, that's why," he said, holding a conversation with himself. "I forgot that she's a maniac who drives a sardine tin on wheels. If I get to the ballpark in one piece I'll never sin again. I promise."

"That promise will last about ten minutes."

"Keep your eyes on the road, for God's sake."

"Sheesh, you're a baby." I took the new exit to the ballpark, shifting down on the ramp.

"Are we there yet?"

"Open your eyes. Lo, before us is the eighth wonder of the world. Look at the size of it! Do you know where I'm supposed to park?"

He directed me towards an out-of-the-way section of the lot, reserved for press. It figured. The box holders couldn't be forced to walk an extra couple of hundred yards to the entrance. No, that was for us, with our computers and briefcases and other assorted crap. I pulled into the best spot I could find.

"Want some help getting out?" I asked Jeff.

He stood up in his seat with his head sticking through the roof to get his legs out, which lost him a bit of dignity. Not that he has much to spare. Aside from his height, Jeff is cursed with a face that, while attractive, features a largish and rather beak-like nose. The overall effect is not unlike a flamingo, though not as pink.

"Okay, kiddo, let's go and make journalism history," Jeff said.

Even though, at forty, I've got almost ten years on him, he always calls me kid. But he has redeeming features. He can write, for a start, and is that rare jock journalist who is neither cynical nor starstruck. Besides, he always laughs at my jokes.

We walked across the parking lot towards the stadium, decked in banners, past recently planted trees and grass that couldn't quite hide the fact that it had been a construction site only weeks before.

We went in the press entrance and, after some confusion over our credentials, took the elevator to the press box. I was glad to see that the Titans had kept the ancient retainer who passes out press notes and keeps strangers away from the place. He showed us where the *Planet* seats were in the opulent new press box.

"No windows!" I said. "Hallelujah."

In the old park, the press box had been sealed in behind glass to keep the elements out. It also kept out crowd sounds and any real excitement in the game being played.

We tried out our new soft swivel chairs, set up our computers, and checked that the phone worked. It was all pretty nice. Looking down on the field, we could see some of the Titans were taking batting practice. Others were gawking like tourists at their new park.

I spotted one of our photographers, but not the one I was looking for. What I wanted was some nice unguarded stuff of Tiny, taking his batting-practice cuts, kidding around with the other players, signing autographs: shots that needed a modicum of sensitivity and imagination. Jay Morse is a good photographer who could handle the assignment easily, but she wasn't here yet.

Bill Spencer, who was, is one of those journeymen who is fine for pictures of lottery winners and car wrecks, but nothing a lot more challenging. His idea of covering a game is to focus one camera on home plate and the other on second base and snap any action that comes into the frame. I hate working with him. Not only is he unprofessional, he gives me the creeps.

The first day he was assigned to one of my stories, he made it clear that he doesn't approve of women reporters, especially women sports reporters. Over the years he has delighted in taking pictures of me with naked athletes in the locker room to show around the newsroom, with rude captions attached. Besides, he smells. I decided to leave him to his clichéd shots of the open roof and wait for Jay to get me the stuff I wanted.

"Coming, beautiful?"

"Keep sweet-talking me and I might, big boy."

When we got to the elevator, Cecil was on duty and, I was glad to see, looking well. He's a man of about seventy who has been in charge of the elevator since I began covering the team six years ago. He's a real gentleman.

"Nice to see you back, Miss Henry," he said.

"And you, too," I said. "You're looking well."

"I'm in the pink, thank you."

"How was your winter?"

"Pretty good. The wife and I went down to Florida."

"Did you get any fishing in, Cec?" asked Jeff. Cross-generational guy talk.

"A little. I'm getting on a bit for that. At least that's what the wife says."

The elevator stopped at the ground floor and the doors slid open.

"Don't you believe it," I said.

"I always say you're only as young as you feel."

"You bet, Cec. See you later."

"Thanks,

"If he's right, I'm about seventy-five," I said as we went into the wide service corridor that ran under the stands. It still showed signs of being under construction. We followed the hand-lettered signs to the tunnel that went past the umpires' locker room to the Titan dugout.

It was busy on the field. Television crews were setting up, officious production assistants giving unnecessary orders to technicians in down vests and jeans. A dozen blow-dried on-air personalities practised their spiels, pointing out the wonders of the stadium.

The Cleveland Indian team bus had just arrived, and the players wandered out of their dugout in street clothes, stopping to chat with former team-mates and old friends and to stare at the tens of thousands of empty blue seats.

The pitchers were in the outfield running sprints. Tiny was in the batting cage, his face grim. Dummy Doran, the bullpen coach, was tossing soft pitches, but Tiny was popping them all up. Sugar Jenkins, the batting coach, and Red O'Brien, the manager, stood behind the cage with crossed arms and expressionless faces.

When his turn was over, Tiny stepped out of the cage and banged his bat on the ground. Alex Jones jumped in to replace him and began spraying sharp hits in all directions.

Sugar took Tiny to one side, and the two conferred in soft voices, the diminutive coach gesturing with his hands as though he held a bat, while the huge first baseman loomed over him, listening. Finally, Tiny shook his head, then made a remark that made both of them laugh. Turning away, I noticed Jay Morse, snapping pictures of the pair with a long lens.

"Great, Jay," I said. "Did Jake tell you what I wanted?"

"No, I just thought we might need some pictures of Washington. Things aren't going very well for him, are they?"

"You've got it right."

I filled her in briefly, and probably unnecessarily, on what I thought we might need, then joined Tiny, who was walking off the field.

"So what did Sugar have to say?"

"Nothing I haven't heard before." He put his bat in the rack and stripped off his gloves, then sat down on the bench, a frown on the dark face that usually only smiled.

"I guess not."

"Have you noticed anything different with my stance lately? I'm not sure my front foot's right."

"You're asking me? You must be desperate. All I can tell you to do is relax."

"I've heard that before, too."

"Don't worry, it will come."

"I'm too old to worry about something I got no control over. I just wish my stroke would come back."

"Me too, Tiny."

" 'Cause if it doesn't, you know that kid's got his bags packed down in Triple A."

He grabbed his glove and trotted out to the infield. Conversation over.

Just then, Joe Kelsey came over to the rack to choose a bat. I greeted him, and he acknowledged me with a brief nod.

"Is something wrong, Joe?"

"We're losing, that's what's wrong."

"Is that all? Are you worried about something? Are you mad at me?"

He shook his head and walked away. I shrugged. Just another day in the big leagues.

CHAPTER

6

By Katherine Henry
Planet Staff

The high point of opening day at the all-new Titan Colosseum yesterday came before the first pitch was thrown. After that, things went downhill fast.

American League President Fulford Covington was on hand to present Titan owner Ted Ferguson with the banner signifying the last year's Eastern Division Championship, the first such pennant for the team.

The ceremonial first pitch was thrown out by Willy Singleton, the first Titan choice in the expansion draft that created the team. Singleton, now a high-school coach in Ardmore, Pennsylvania, threw a strike, something he rarely did while in Titan uniform.

Then things began getting ugly, on the field and in the stands. It was the Cleveland Indians that looked like champions yesterday afternoon, thumping the Titans, 7–2. The only bright spot for the fans was the home run by first baseman Tiny Washington that accounted for both Titan runs. Washington also had a double and single, indicating that he has broken out of the slump he's been struggling with since....

"Attention, scribes. There will be a press conference in the lunchroom in fifteen minutes."

The announcement, by Titan public relations director Hugh Marsh, drew groans from us all.

"What is it, Hugh?"

"Ted and Red will be making the announcement."

"Come on, give us a break."

Marsh is new, and he is a disaster. He's a former vice-president of the brewery that sponsors the Titan broadcasts. He is also an avid baseball fan and statistics nut who decided to take early retirement and live out all his fantasies by working for a baseball team. He loves crunching his numbers and hanging around the ball players, but he hasn't quite got a handle on his role or that of the press in the greater scheme of things. He hasn't quite figured out that he is there to help us, not the other way around. Without us, he wouldn't have a job to do, but is he grateful? Forget it. He treats me the way he probably treated his secretaries in the corporate world.

Still, this time it wasn't too bad. With an afternoon game, my deadline was far enough away that I didn't care about the delay. I got up from my seat and stretched the kinks out of my back. There was no point in continuing with the game story. Whatever Fric and Frac were about to announce could end up being more important than the score of the game.

"Want to come get a coffee, sweetie?"

Jeff, in the throes of his usual struggle to find a lead, shook his head.

When I got to the lunchroom, Ted Ferguson, the owner, was already there, pouring himself a cup of coffee.

"Well, Kate, how are you?"

He didn't offer me a cup, so I poured my own.

"What's this all about? Your public information representative wasn't willing to go public with any information. Which appears to be a contradiction in terms."

"Don't be hard on him Kate. He'll learn."

"If he farts around like this on deadline, he'll learn fast," I grumbled.

"If you don't like the way we run things around here, you can always go cover another team," Ferguson said.

"Thanks a whole lot, Ted. But this isn't a joke. You've got to explain to him that our coverage is important and that he's got to be more helpful."

"No one else is complaining, Kate."

"Which means what, roughly translated, Ted? I'm just some uppity broad who doesn't know her place?"

"You said it, Kate, not me. But I'll see what I can do."

He smiled, showing me lots of caps, then turned away. Just then, Red O'Brien came into the room, followed by Marsh and most of the other reporters.

"Thank you for coming," Ferguson said, as soon as we had settled into seats around the formica tables. "Red has a brief announcement to make, and then we'll open it up for questions. We thought perhaps you might want to talk with us about the season so far. Red?"

He cleared his throat, then scowled.

"We have optioned the contract of utility infielder Bill Stearns to our Triple A affiliate and will replace him on the roster with first baseman Harold Cooper. He'll be here later tonight. Any questions?"

The innocuous announcement was the beginning of the end of Tiny Washington's career.

"I take it this decision was reached before today's game," I said. "Tiny Washington went three for four. Does that make any difference?"

"The decision had nothing to do with Tiny," Red said. "The kid deserves a chance."

"Will Cooper be playing first base tomorrow?"

"Yes, he will. There's no point having him on the bench. For the time being, Washington will be the designated hitter."

"Have you told Tiny?"

"I informed him after the game."

One of the Cleveland writers asked Red about the poor start the Titans were having and half the local reporters got up and broke for the elevators. I didn't bother. I knew they wouldn't have made the announcement until Tiny had left the ballpark. I had his home number. I told Roger Chan to bring me quotes from the other players, then went back to the press box and got on the phone.

Cooper was en route and unavailable and Tiny wasn't home yet. I talked to Jake and promised him a lengthy sidebar on the changes. Then I called Andy.

"I'm working tonight after all," I said. "At least for a while."

"Why didn't you just say you couldn't? Is baseball more important to you than our relationship?"

It took me a second to realize that he was joking.

"Piss off."

"I'm working, too," he laughed. "If I don't see you later, I'll call."

"Everything okay?"

"Crazy and frustrating, mainly. I'll talk to you later."

Hanging up, I looked at the game story, realized I didn't have to change much, and got back to work.

... indicating that he has finally broken out of his season-long slump.

However, that didn't influence the decision of the Titan brass to call up Harold "Kid" Cooper from their Triple A affiliate and hand him Washington's job ....

CHAPTER

7

I was done well before deadline. Kid Cooper arrived in Toronto on a 7:00 flight and I talked to him as soon as he got to his hotel. He was thrilled, of course. He's a big farm boy from Kansas who looks and sounds like a player from a simpler, more innocent era in the game. By the time he's eligible for his first arbitration hearing, he'll probably be another snotty greedhead, but for now he'd look good on a Norman Rockwell cover.

Tiny was philosophical, as I expected him to be. While claiming that he had several good seasons left once he got his stroke straightened out, he had nothing but good wishes for his replacement. There was some poignant irony in the contrast between the eagerness of the young player and the resignation of the older, and the piece just about wrote itself. I tried to avoid the baseball-as-a-metaphor-for-life bullshit, but some of it inevitably crept in. Jake dug through some old photo contact sheets and found shots of Washington and Cooper together when the young player was called up the previous September. With Jay's shots from that afternoon, it made a nice spread.

His attention to Cooper was typical of Tiny. He had known full well that his career was winding down, as he had known who his successor would be. But that didn't stop him from spending time with Cooper, giving him batting and fielding tips, and helping him get used to the big league life.

I was pleased with the piece when I was finished. For all the help Tiny had been to me, I wanted to do him justice, and I thought I had. I went back over his career as a Titan, their first real star after expansion, and recalled what he had meant to the team over the years. It read like an obituary. I'd look like a right chump if Cooper didn't work out and Tiny was back at first base in a week.

I got home at about 10:00. I fed Elwy, checked my machine for nonexistent messages, changed into jeans, grabbed the bottle of bubbly out of the fridge, and went downstairs and knocked on Sally's door.

"Hi, neighbour. Care to take part in a scientific experiment?" I explained about the silver spoon theory of champagne.

"Come on in. You're just in time to say good night to T.C. He's dying to see you."

Her eleven-year-old son is one of my favourite people of any age, the closest I'm likely to get to having a kid of my own. He came to the door with a grin on his face, dressed in his usual gear – jeans and a Titan sweatshirt, his running shoes unlaced and flopping. His big glasses give him an owlish look. He hugged me – a real bonus. Lately he's been getting too big for such foolishness, but I guess a two-month separation is worth an exception.

"What's new, aside from the foot you've grown since I saw you last?"

T.C. looked at his sneakers.

"What do you mean? I've still just got two."

"Ha ha ha."

"How's Tiny? Did you see that home run he hit today?"

I winced. Tiny was T.C.'s hero. He had taken a great interest in the boy since they first met. I think T.C. sleeps with a home-run bat Tiny gave him during the pennant stretch, and having a friend like Tiny gives him some needed status in the schoolyard.

"He's not great, T.C. They're bringing Cooper up to play first base tomorrow."

"Oh, shit," he said, with a combination of embarrassment and defiance over his choice of words. "That's not fair. He's started to hit again. They can't bench him."

"He won't be going anywhere. They're going to DH him until they see what Cooper can do. I talked to Tiny. He said it will give him a chance to concentrate on hitting, so maybe it's not too bad. Besides, Cooper's a nice guy, too."

"I still think it stinks."

"So do I, kid. So do I."

"If I write him a letter, will you take it to him?"

"Sure, but isn't it a bit late?"

"Can I, Mum?" An ogre with a stone for a heart couldn't have refused him.

"Make it quick," she said.

He ran to his bedroom and I followed Sally to the kitchen, the most comfortable room in her apartment. While she got out the wine glasses, I hunted up her only ashtray in a cluttered cupboard and shifted a stack of books, mail, and tools to the shelf behind the table.

"Wait, I need that screwdriver," Sally said. "And the wrench. I'm fixing this tap."

Sally's a great tenant, because she's a crack handywoman. She's not always prompt, mind you, but she knows how to do things once she gets around to them. The kitchen tap had leaked before I went to Florida.

"Can I help?"

She laughed.

Having made the offer, I sat down and poured the wine. This silver spoon trick actually worked. There was some fizz left twenty-four hours after it had been opened. Sally worked efficiently, muttering to herself, and occasionally to me. I smoked and watched the performance, while giving her the news of my time in Florida and my aborted reunion with Andy.

"My life would be a whole lot less complicated if I didn't share it with a cop."

"Are you and Andy fighting again? You shouldn't do that," said T.C., who had come into the kitchen, shaking his head disapprovingly. Sometimes this kid acted like my older brother.

"Nothing serious, you precocious little creep."

"You're not going to break up with him, are you?"

"No such luck. Is that the letter?"

He handed me a sealed envelope.

"I marked it 'Personal,'" he said.

"And Kate and I are going to steam it open the minute you go to bed," said Sally, from under the sink. "Which is right now, sport."

"Aw, Mum. Can't I just talk to Kate for a while?"

"Not on a school night, with a test tomorrow."

"Wait, wait, let me just tell her about Thursday."

He didn't pause for permission.

"My class is going on a field trip to the *Planet*."

"Your tour will go right behind my desk, then. I've got schoolkids breathing down my neck half the time I'm in there. Don't throw spitballs at me, okay?"

"Can I introduce you to some of my friends?"

"If I'm there when you get there. I don't spend a lot of time at the office."

He looked disappointed.

"All right, all right. Are you coming in the morning or afternoon?"

"Morning."

"I'll try to be there."

"You promise?"

"I promise," I sighed. "Of course, you won't mind if I call you Toodles in front of your friends."

"You wouldn't," he said. "You wouldn't dare!"

"Not if you mind your Ps and Qs until then, buster."

"Like going to bed *tout de suite*," Sally said.

"Give me a smooch first, handsome."

He pecked me on the cheek, then patted his mother's bum, which was the only part of her available, and wished us good night. He winked at me as he left the room.

"He's turning into a smartass," Sally said, crawling out from her cave, but the affection in her eyes betrayed her. She stood up and turned the water on, then off, with satisfaction. No drip.

I applauded and she curtsied, a fairly ludicrous gesture from one dressed in a leopard-print jumpsuit, then plopped herself down at the table and reached for her glass.

"Adolescence is looming," she said. "I can feel us sinking into a decade of turmoil."

"He's not even twelve yet," I laughed.

"They start early now," she said. "It's their diet or something."

"I don't think you have to worry."

"I wish I could believe you," she said, suddenly serious. "He got caught shoplifting while you were away."

"You're kidding!"

"He and a bunch of kids from school went down to Gerrard Square and hit one of the jeans stores. Luckily the cops called the parents rather than lay charges. I hope T.C. had his criminal streak scared right out of him. I thought maybe Andy could talk to him."

"I'll ask. But I don't think it's anything to get bent out of shape over. Every kid does it sometime. Didn't you?"

"Never."

"Gee, I was part of a gang of desperados who used to steal a candy bar every day on the way home from school for a while. One of us would buy something as a diversion and the rest would help ourselves. I feel guilty about it to this day."

"But your father was a minister," she gasped.

"That's why I had to prove that I could be as naughty as the next kid."

"I'm shocked!"

"But I didn't end up a crook for life, and neither will T.C. He was probably lucky he got caught."

"I guess."

"Lucky he encountered a decent cop. Or lucky he's a nice, white, middle-class kid the cops call parents about. Anyway, I'll see what Andy has to say."

"Speaking of which, where is he tonight?"

"Working. He's on these child murders. I don't think I'll be seeing much of him until they're solved."

"I hope he gets the guy soon, for my sake as well as yours. These kids are T.C.'s age. This whole thing is giving me nightmares."

"You don't have to worry about T.C.," I reassured her. "He's smart and he's street-proofed."

"I hope so."

"Are they talking about it at his school?"

"Sure, they had a policeman in talking to the assembly after the second murder."

"And you've talked about it at home."

"Of course. But I'm still worried about him. I can't be here all the time. I'm even thinking about taking a leave from the gallery to look after him."

"As your landlady, I wouldn't advise it," I laughed. "Besides, whether you're here or not, T.C. is too smart to go off with some fast-talking stranger."

"Maybe it wasn't a stranger. We don't know."

"For God's sake, stop worrying about it. He's a solid, level-headed kid."

"Sure, a level-headed kid who runs around with hoodlums after school."

"Relax. Have another glass of bubbly."

"Don't mind if I do."

I poured.

"So, what else is new?" I asked.

"A man."

"Another starving artist?"

Sally was notorious for choosing losers. Her last one had done very bizarre performance art and neglected to return money he borrowed.

"No, this one is pretty straight. His name is David Pelham, he's forty-two, and he's been divorced for five years. No children or other encumbrances. I met him at a fund-raiser for the African National Congress."

"What does he do?"

"He's a social worker. He counsels troubled kids. He's really nice."

"So maybe he can help straighten around your wayward son."

"I don't think T.C. is quite ready to take David's advice."

"Oh, it's like that, is it? A little bit of jealousy from your pre-pubescent son?"

"Just a touch."

"How long has this been going on?"

"Do you realize that you are sounding more and more like my mother every day?"

"Yes, dear. And by the way, what does his father do?"

"He's a Mountie."

"Gack!"

"I told you he was straight," Sally laughed. "But, mercifully, not as straight as his dad. And I've been seeing him for a month."

"Well, here's to you, then," I said, hoisting my glass. "I hope I get to meet him soon. I'll want to give my blessing before it goes too far. Or am I too late for that?"

"Actually, no," she said. "It's a little strange, but we haven't actually done it yet."

"Done it? As in capital-Done, capital-It?"

"He says he doesn't want to rush into anything. I guess he's old-fashioned."

"Or not as straight as you think," I said.

"I'm not worried about that," Sally said, somewhat demurely. "He is definitely heterosexual."

"Oh, you have progressed to heavy petting then."

"Kate, you are terrible."

"The state my sex life is in these days, I have to get my kicks vicariously."

CHAPTER

8

The phone was ringing when I got upstairs. I picked it up as the machine answered and yelled into it over my own recorded voice. The machine was attached to the phone in my study on the third floor and wasn't affected when I picked up the kitchen extension.

"I'll talk after the beep," I said. "Don't hang up. I'm really here."

I was laughing by the time the message finished and the beep sounded.

"All right, you bum," I said. "What's your excuse this time?"

"Kate?"

The voice wasn't Andy's.

"It's Joe Kelsey."

"Joe, what's up?"

"I need to talk to you."

I looked at my watch. It was almost midnight.

"Now?"

"I want some advice," Joe said.

"What's wrong?"

"Nothing's wrong. I just have a story for you. It's a scoop, I guess you call it."

He laughed.

"Joe, what is this about?"

"I've decided I want to tell a story, and you're the one I want to tell it to."

His voice was interrupted by the beep signalling another call on the line. I apologized to Joe, and switched lines. It was Andy, still at work. I told him I adored him and would see him the next day, and got back to Joe.

"Sorry. What's the story, Joe?"

"I'd rather tell it to your face. Can we come over?"

"Who is we?"

"There's a friend I want you to meet."

"I take it this can't wait until tomorrow?"

"We can be there in fifteen minutes."

"Hey, what else have I got to do? Just go to bed and get a decent night's sleep for a change. Sure. Come on over. But it had better be good."

Maybe I was going to find out what had been on Joe's mind all spring. I just hoped it wasn't going to be a repeat of one bizarre occasion in Cleveland when Joe tried to save my soul. Oh, Lord, what if he was bringing another Holy Roller with him for a spot of sharing of scripture? I wasn't in the mood. I doubted it, though. I hadn't been very receptive the last time, after all, and we'd stayed friends. Who knows? He might just want to dump all over his team-mates, or demand a trade, or something else that would be good copy.

I did a quick tidy of the parts of the place that my visitors were likely to see, throwing debris into the bedroom. Elwy grumped at me when I moved the pile of newspapers he'd been lying on, then waddled to the kitchen to sniff at his food dish. I got a notebook from my study and put a fresh cassette in the recorder I use for long interviews. When Joe knocked on the door, the kettle was just coming to the boil.

He looked more relaxed than I'd seen him in weeks. With him was a good-looking man in his thirties, well-dressed and fit, his hair brown with just a hint of grey. They dropped their jackets on a chair in the hall, then followed me to the kitchen. We decided upon tea, and made small talk while I brewed it. Joe's friend, Sandy Montgomery, turned out to be a lawyer from San Francisco, across the bay from Joe's home town, Oakland. He was making his first visit to Toronto.

"I hope you're enjoying it," I said, as we settled in at the kitchen table.

"I'm having a great time," he said, smiling broadly.

"Maybe I'd better explain," Joe said, looking a little nervous. "Sandy's not just a friend. He's my lover."

I only spilled a bit of the tea I was pouring. I looked from Joe to his friend, who watched me with some amusement in his eyes. It was he who broke the silence. I wasn't about to.

"I guess you're surprised because I'm white," he said.

Joe began to laugh, and the two of them slapped palms, exchanging fives. I had to laugh too, albeit a little nervously.

"And where do I come in?"

"We want you to write about it," Joe said.

"We're sick of hiding," Sandy explained, a little belligerently. "Joe and I think the world is ready for a gay baseball player. You don't?"

"I don't have a lot of problem with it, personally," I said, carefully, "but I'm not your average baseball-type person. In a word, no, I don't think that world is ready."

"Will it ever be?" Sandy asked. "It wasn't that long ago that baseball wasn't ready for a black player either."

"True enough, but does Joe want to be the Jackie Robinson of this particular cause? Have you really thought this through, Joe? If you go through with it, you'd better consider the consequences."

"I've hardly done anything else for the past few months," Joe said. "I know that it won't be easy, but it's something I have to do. You should understand that better than anyone. You know that Sultan Sanchez was blackmailing me. Every time I paid him, I thought about what would happen if the word got out."

Kelsey had been a suspect in Sanchez's murder because of the blackmail material the Dominican had left behind, including a clipping which listed Joe as a found-in in a bath-house raid in Knoxville. Charges were eventually dropped, but Sultan, not a particularly nice person, found out, and hit Joe for a couple of grand a month. Joe didn't have much choice.

Even though I had known about Joe's past through my involvement in the Titan murders – the blackmail material had been sent to me – I was surprised by his visit for a couple of reasons. Preacher came by his nickname honestly. He was the most devout of the born-again Christians on the team, not the most sexually enlightened group around. I always assumed that he had embraced his faith so fervently to slay his homosexual demons.

But even if he had managed to come to terms with himself, I was amazed that he was ready to go public. His peers were going to despise him. As for the fans, who could know, but it wasn't going to be easy.

"I think you're nuts," I said.

"Since I've been with Sandy, I've decided that I can handle any kind of abuse, as long as we're together."

They smiled at each other. I looked away.

"It's going to come from everywhere, Preacher. Can you imagine the fans in Yankee Stadium?"

"I'm looking forward to Detroit, myself," Sandy chuckled. "The bleacher creatures are going to be freaked."

The guy was beginning to get on my nerves. It wasn't him they were going to be throwing things at.

"What about your own team-mates, then? You have a hard enough time with some of them just because you're black. Have you thought about Stinger Swain's reaction?"

Swain, the third baseman, was a vicious racist and sexist with a large repertoire of faggot jokes.

"He already treats me like dogshit, Kate. How could it get any worse?"

"We're talking about a very conservative bunch of guys, Joe, you know that. I don't want to be rude here, but even the nicest ones aren't going to want to share the shower with you once this story is published. You're going to lose friends."

"Who is this bitch?" Sandy got up from the table and began to pace. "I thought you said she'd understand."

"I told you, I don't have any problem with it myself. I'm happy for you, Joe, if you are. But I just want to make sure you know what you're in for."

"Cool it, Sandy," Joe said. "She's trying to help."

"One more thing, then I'll shut up. What about the church? That's been an awfully important part of your life. Are you ready for them to shut the door in your face?"

Preacher sat quietly for a moment.

"That's what has kept me from admitting I'm gay all this time," he said. "I turned to Jesus to help me deny that I'm this way. But it didn't work. And all around me I saw hatred of what I am. *I* hated what I am. But I don't hate it any more. Sandy has helped me. We both belong to a small gay congregation at home. I've made my peace with Jesus. If the church can't make peace with me, that's their problem."

I poured more tea while I thought. He was certainly sincere. Joe's a grown man. I thought he was being naive, but nothing I could say would change his mind. If he wanted to come out of the locker, as it were, I couldn't stop him.

Besides, it was a great story. I'd wondered for a long time how gay players coped. And you know there have to be gay players hidden in locker rooms all over both leagues. This was going to be interesting.

"Okay, let's do it," I said. "You're right, it's quite a story. Do you want to start now or wait?"

"I'm ready to talk now, if it's not too late for you. I'd like to get it over with."

What followed wasn't that unusual a love story, except for its context. When it was published it would be a bombshell, but in the small hours of a Wednesday morning it was rather sweet.

Joe told me about his confusion as an adolescent, his attraction to men, and his denial of it. Again, not a new story. When he was playing in the minor leagues he went to the gay baths to see what it was all about.

He never found out, ironically, because the joint was raided shortly after he got there and he had to confront what it would cost him if his team-mates or the Titan organization had found out. It scared him, if not straight, celibate. It also sent him into the born-again fold and five years of extreme self-loathing.

Then came the blackmail, of course. When Sanchez was murdered, Kelsey was relieved. But he still felt vulnerable. There were new people who knew about it, for one thing: the police, me. And who else?

"I worried about it until I was sick," he said. "Then I realized that one of the things bothering me was that I didn't know for sure whether I was gay. I decided to find out."

It wasn't hard to know where to start. He took the bridge across San Francisco Bay and went into the first gay bookstore he came to. He bought a guide and found the upscale health club where he met Sandy.

"It's a really nice place, Kate. I had thought these places were kind of seamy, you know, like that club in Knoxville. I was pretty scared. And all the AIDS stuff kind of freaked me out."

"That was the first lecture I gave him," Sandy said.

"I spent the winter doing my training there," Joe continued. "It was just like any other club, except that I didn't have to pretend."

Sandy smiled.

"But he was, you will pardon the expression, the belle of the ball," he said. "He's a celebrity, after all. A major leaguer in a town that loves baseball. Joe didn't lack for invitations."

Kelsey laughed.

"Yes, but only one mattered. Sandy has opened a whole new world to me. It's like going to college. My new friends talk about things I'd never thought about before. I don't mean sex. Books, politics, stuff like that. I'm not used to talking about anything but baseball. None of the guys on the team are very interested in what goes on in the world."

"Tell me about it," I said.

The three of us laughed like old friends. I poured more tea.

CHAPTER

9

Sandy and Joe left just after 2:00. They seemed very happy together. I had twinges of suspicion that Sandy might be using Joe for his own political purposes, but he seemed genuinely fond of him, and willing to stand by him if things got ugly. The change in Joe was remarkable. I'd never seen him so at ease. He had lost his shyness and gained confidence.

Selfishly, I asked them to promise to keep quiet for a few more days. I wanted time to put together a blockbuster for the Saturday paper with its half-million circulation. Hey, if I'm going to get a scoop, it might as well be a big one. I needed time to discuss the handling of the story with Jake and get some photographs. Sandy also agreed to stay out of sight until the weekend.

I slept through my first alarm in the morning, but had set a backup across the room, and was at the

Planet by 10:00. Jake knew the story by a quarter past. He looked at me, stunned, for a few seconds, then broke into a smile.

"National Newspaper Award, for sure," he said. "I knew putting a broad on the beat would pay off one day."

"Thanks for the recognition of my talents," I said. "How do you want to play it?"

" The happy couple will pose for pictures?"

"As far as I know. I thought we could send Jay. She can keep her mouth shut."

"I wonder if they'll hold hands. That would be cute."

And Jake is what passes for an enlightened guy in this business.

"Do you need any sidebars or anything?" I asked. "I suppose I could do something on homosexuality in sport, but I don't really feel like phoning around for it this week. The more people I talk to about this, the better chance that we'll lose the exclusive."

"That's all right," Jake said. "Let's not dilute the impact of what we've got. We can do that stuff afterwards, while the rest of the papers are matching our story. I expect there's going to be a lot of pretty heavy reaction, too."

"I guess that's the end of my weekend off," I said.

"Why? I'll just send one of the kids out to cover the team reaction. I'm sure Roger will be able to handle it."

"Bastard. Just get someone else to do the game stories."

"Starting tonight. I don't want you near the team until Saturday."

"Thanks. I have enough to do."

I was at the door when Jake stopped me.

"Be sure you find out which one's the wife."

I left without answering, my high spirits dampened. The story was a great coup for me, but Joe was leaving himself open for a lot of crap, even from people like Jake.

I settled in at my desk for a day of slogging. The first job was to transcribe a couple of hours' worth of tapes. I found the departmental tape recorder easily enough, but it took me half an hour to track down the earphones, which had been borrowed by the entertainment department, and the foot pedal, which turned up in the business section.

Then I had to put up with chirping from the next desk.

"We haven't had that beer yet, Kate. How about it?"

"I've been pretty busy, Dickie. Maybe later today, if I can get through this."

"What are you working on?"

"A feature for the weekend."

"What's it about?"

"Sorry, Dickie. I can't talk about it right now."

"Well, excuse me for living," he said. "I'll catch you later, when you're not involved in top-secret projects."

He made one of those obnoxious pistol gestures with his index finger, shot me, winked, and went back to the phones.

By the end of the afternoon I had a backache from hunching over the keyboard and eyestrain from looking at the screen, but I had finished transcribing. I took a printout to work on at home, then used a security feature of our computer system to put the whole thing in code. There are hackers in the newsroom who spend most of their shifts figuring out passwords and browsing through other people's files.

I signed out of the system and told Dickie, tied to his desk by phone calls from his high-school correspondents, that we'd have that beer real soon.

I was just about out of there when Jake grabbed me and marched me in to see Ron Wilson, the Managing Editor. He wanted the story to run on the front page – big deal – instead of in the sports section, so he had to get into the act.

His office was on a direct diagonal across the newsroom from the sports section, but we had to thread our way through an obstacle course of little gatherings of work stations representing the various departments. We turned right at Entertainment, left at Foreign, right again at Business, and left past the feature writers into his outer office.

I could see him at his desk, gazing out the window while he played with a paper clip. Wilson is a little man, not much older than I, who works with his jacket off so everyone can admire his old-fashioned sleeve garters. He would wear a green eyeshade, too, if he didn't think people would laugh.

Jake rapped on the door jamb. Wilson turned, saw us, and jumped from his chair and strode across the room. He shook my hand conspiratorially.

"What a bombshell! Out of the closet and into the locker room," he said, by way of greeting.

"I trust you're not writing the head," I said.

"Great story, Kate, just great," he said. "It will sell a lot of papers."

Oh, Joe will be so pleased, I thought.

"There's going to be a lot of interest in you, too," he said. "I thought maybe you might do a first-person piece about how you got the story. How 'bout that?"

I looked at Jake, who was trying to keep a straight face.

"He just handed it to me," I said. "I didn't do anything to get it. I'm not really comfortable writing in the first person."

"But a scoop like this deserves something extra," he said. "See if you can't work a little personal angle into it in your section, Jake."

"We'll see what we can do," Jake said, as we edged towards the door.

"A world copyright exclusive, by our Katie. Way to go! Keep in touch."

"I think our Katie deserves a drink," Jake muttered as we made our way back across the newsroom. "My treat."

"Let me just call Andy first," I said. "We're supposed to be meeting for supper."

"I'll catch you downstairs, then."

"Order me a scotch."

CHAPTER

10

The Final Edition, the bar and restaurant on the main floor of the *Planet* building was packed, usual at the end of the day. But no one was eating. The food is terrible. *Planet* staffers have been known to warn off unwary tourists who blunder in after a day at Harbourfront. It's just our way of helping Toronto's world-class image. The Ministry of Tourism and Recreation should give us an award.

Jake had grabbed a table in the middle of the room, surrounded by the usual collection of complainers drinking away a day of ego-busting. At the reporters' tables they were whining about the stifling of creativity. The editors, at their own tables, talked about the decline in standards of journalism. Sometimes the cocktail hour ended in fist fights. Other times, the two factions joined together in sloppy camaraderie. The later it was in the week, the wilder it got. This was Thursday night. I manoeuvred myself into one of the bucket chairs brought in during the most recent renovation and looked around.

I cringed when I saw who was at the next table. Bill Spencer was centre stage, showing off his collection of photographs. As well as snapping me in action, he also specialized in getting disgusting pictures of famous people: the mayor with his finger up his nose, the prime minister adjusting his crotch, that sort of thing.

From what I could see, he was showing off windy-day shots. Most photographers loathe weather assignments, but Spencer, who got more than his share, loved them. Windy days mean skirts over the head, of course, and he had collected hundreds of crotch shots of hapless secretaries over the years.

"Don't these people have homes to go to?" I asked.

Jake laughed.

"Since you hooked up with that cop, you've forgotten the rituals of your profession. For shame."

"Where's my drink?"

"I haven't managed to get Lenore's attention yet," he said, flailing a wild semaphore across the room. It worked.

"Sorry, love, what'll it be," said the fiftyish waitress, wiping the table with a rag. Her hair is always bleached blonde, she wears a pointy bra under a tight white sweater, and behaves as either a mother or a bouncer, whichever is most appropriate.

Jake stroked her skinny bum in its polyester mini-skirt.

"A pair of scotches," he said. "Johnny Walker Red, not your watered-down bar shit."

"Keep your hands to yourself or you'll get nothing, buster," she said.

"Go get him, Lenore," I said, "but since I am not sexually harassing you, it would be right sisterly if you would bring my drink. I try my best to keep these guys in line, but they're so old, they can't change their mentality."

"They're so old, all they can do is touch anyway," she said, slipping expertly between the jammed tables.

"She got you, Jake," I said. "And, semi-seriously, you really should keep your hands off her. How would you like it if Ron Wilson pinched you on the cheek whenever you came up with a good idea in the features meeting?"

"Come on, Kate. Lenore and I are old friends. She understands."

"She probably does, but she might like you better if you weren't like all the rest of the pigs in the bar. Besides, you're likely to get a drink in your lap one of these days."

Lenore, bless her heart, had done just that to one of the more obnoxious representatives of the rewrite desk a few weeks before. It was the talk of the newsroom.

When she returned to our table with a loaded tray, my scotch was noticeably larger than Jake's. I raised one eyebrow at him, a trick I perfected at university after spending more hours practising it in front of my mirror than studying at my desk. I flunked out, but I have a devastating eyebrow.

"Thank you very much, Lenore," he said, reaching into his pocket and putting a crumpled handful of bills on the tray.

"Don't mention it," she said, with a smug smile. Turning, she almost collided with Dickie Greaves.

"Get me a Blue," he said, then snagged an empty chair and pulled it up to our table, oblivious to the fact that he was blocking an aisle.

"This is a break, finding you both here," he said, with his best boyish smile. "I hope I'm not interrupting anything."

"No, not at all," Jake said, downing his drink. "I was just leaving. You can keep Kate company."

I glared at him. He reached over, pinched my cheek, and told me he'd see me tomorrow.

"Perhaps," I said.

Dickie moved into Jake's chair, and started to push the other one back to its proper table.

"Leave it," I said. "A friend of mine should be joining us in a few minutes."

"Who? Don't tell me I'm going to meet Staff Sergeant Munro?" he asked. I nodded.

"That's great," he said. "I've been wanting to meet the man who has broken the hearts of the entire sports department by stealing you away."

"Give it a rest, Dickie. Practise your charm on another victim. I'm old enough to be your mother, and you're married already. How's the baby?"

"He's just great. He can roll over."

"And Beth? How is she liking motherhood?"

"I think she's getting the hang of it."

"And are you a good modern father? Diaper detail and all that?"

He smiled uncomfortably and ran his fingers through his well-cut hair. He looked around for his beer before answering.

"Well, I'm pretty busy with work, of course.

That stuff is Beth's department. She doesn't want me messing around with it."

"But you've already given him his first baseball glove, right?"

"Darn straight."

We were laughing when Andy appeared in the door. I waved. Dickie craned his neck around and watched Andy cross the room. So did I. I never get tired of looking at this man. He is slight, but strong, with dark curly hair, strong cheekbones and jaw, and gentle grey eyes. He's a knockout, in my eyes. He looked tired, but sexy.

"Hi, darling. I've saved you a chair," I said. "I'd like you to meet a colleague of mine. . . ."

Dickie jumped up and stuck out his hand.

"Richard Greaves," he said. "It's a great honour to meet you. I'm an admirer of your work."

"*Richard* is in charge of our school sports section," I explained.

"How interesting," Andy said. He looked around for service. Lenore, spotting an interesting new face, was at his side in a flash.

"I'd love a martini," he said.

"Not here, you wouldn't," Lenore answered. "Stick to the straight stuff."

"She's right. She watches out for her friends. So I'd better introduce you. Andy, this is Lenore, who is the protector of all innocents who enter here. Lenore, this is my friend Andy Munro."

Andy rose halfway from his chair and shook her hand.

"I'll have whatever Kate's having, thanks," he said. "And Richard?"

"I ordered a Blue ten minutes ago," he grumbled.

"But you didn't say 'please,'" Lenore shot back over her shoulder.

"Pretty please with sugar on it," said Dickie, his hands steepled as in prayer.

Andy looked around the room, barely keeping a straight face. He had never seen the bar at full tilt before. It was a sight. The (male) foreign editor was arm wrestling with the (female) business columnist at one table, while a bunch of transplanted Brits sang dirty rugger songs at the next.

In the darkest corner a pair of middle-aged copy editors were coming as close as possible to sex in public without getting arrested for it. Andy smiled, insincerely, and turned to Dickie.

"What does your job involve? High school? Minor hockey? Little league?"

"All of it. I find covering amateur athletics far more rewarding than the crass commercialism of professional sports."

Sure, and he would sell his first-born for a chance at the hockey beat. Lenore came back with the drinks. I took out my wallet.

"Nope, they're paid for," she said.

"Jake?"

"Not a chance," she said, pointing a few tables over. When we looked, Margaret Papadakis raised her glass at us. At Andy.

There was no graceful way out of it. I smiled and raised my glass at her.

"Wasn't that nice?" Andy said. "I must return the favour sometime."

I was about to kick him under the table when Dickie carried on the conversation as if there had been no interruption.

"But what I do is nothing compared to your work," he said to Andy. "It's so important. My father was a cop up north. I thought of joining myself, but I didn't have what it takes. I'm not tough enough."

"Most of it is just paperwork," Andy said, not comfortable with the turn of conversation.

"These murders you're working on are horrifying. I know the brother of one of the boys. The family is devastated."

"Really? Which one?" I asked.

"Benny Goldman. I did a feature on his brother Justin's hockey team last winter. I talked to Justin's mother last week, extended my condolences. It's a terrible thing. Have you found any suspects?"

"I'm really not at liberty to discuss it," Andy said, looking to me for help.

"Let's talk about something more cheerful," I said, dutifully.

"They have to be connected, don't they? All these murders?" Dickie wasn't going to let it go.

"That's the assumption we're working on," said Andy, gone all stuffy and cop-like.

"A serial killer, right here in Toronto. I thought that only happened in the States."

"What about Clifford Olson?" I said. "He was Canadian. And that guy in New Brunswick. It looks like we're catching up to our violent neighbours to the south."

"Maybe there are others we don't even know about," Dickie said. "How sophisticated are your computers?"

"We progressed beyond stone tablets and chisels a few years ago," Andy said, drily.

"I don't mean to insult you," Dickie said. "I was

reading an article about serial killers the other day. It said that until recently if a killer murdered people in different provinces or even different cities, the police wouldn't necessarily realize that they were connected."

"That article is way out of date," Andy said. "Maybe a few years ago that would have happened, both in the States and here. But not now. Now we would connect the crimes."

"Listen, if there is anything I can do to help, since I know the family, just call me."

"Certainly. Thanks for your offer," Andy said, then downed his drink.

"I'm really sorry to have to break this up, but we have dinner reservations. I'd love to talk longer, but you know how it is in Toronto restaurants these days."

"Absolutely," I said, gathering up my things. "They'll blackball you for life if you don't show up on time."

We said our goodbyes and got out of there as quickly as we could. Andy had to stop by Margaret's table to thank her. I gave her a particularly generous smile as we left. After all, he was leaving with me.

When the door closed behind us, I grabbed Andy's sleeve and kissed him. After he had stopped responding, we both laughed.

"Never again, I promise. I'll meet you anywhere but here," he said.

"It's a deal," I agreed. "So, where are these hot reservations? Somewhere dark and romantic, I hope."

"I know a spot in Riverdale where you can get

superb pasta with an intimate, homey ambience. Chez Katarina."

"Let's take both cars. I'll toss you for who stops for the pasta and who makes the martinis."

I just made it for closing time at Sanelli's, the Italian deli in the yuppie health-food mall that caters to lazy cooks who don't like tofu. I talked the sullen teenager behind the counter into selling me fettucini and some red clam sauce. I went to the cheese store down the street for a hunk of parmesan to grate, then stopped at Sunland for salad stuff and some spring flowers.

As I climbed the stairs to my door, I heard music playing and what sounded like conversation. Pausing outside, I realized that Andy was talking to Elwy. As I opened the door, they were discussing my lateness.

"Caught you," I laughed. "Big tough cop, conversing with a cat. What would your macho buddies say?"

"Well, there was no one else to talk to," he grumbled. "Right, Elwy? She's hanging around the

Danforth flirting with handsome Greeks and forgets the two of us waiting at home for dinner, starving."

Andy took the bags from me and unpacked them while I arranged irises and daffodils in an old-fashioned milk bottle on the kitchen table. Then I attended to Elwy, who tried to eat the food while I was still glopping it out of the can into his bowl.

"I put the martini glasses in the freezer if you're still up for it," he said.

"I could handle a small one. But first I'm going to get out of these clothes."

I went into the bedroom and grabbed my most comfortable sweats. I continued the conversation loudly enough to carry to the kitchen.

"You seem pretty cheerful."

"I can't imagine why," Andy called. "For sure, it's not because of the day I had. Probably because it's over."

"And it certainly can't have anything to do with my company," I said, coming back into the room.

"Not dressed like that," he said, kissing me as he handed me the drink. "When women go away to slip into something comfortable, they're supposed to reappear dressed in slinky and black. You looked sexier in your work clothes. You're taking me for granted, woman."

"And you keep coming back for more."

"Actually," he said, dropping a piece of clam on the floor, "it's Elwy I can't do without."

It was nice to have an evening at home, back to the easy domesticity we'd enjoyed in the off-season. The only change was that I listened with one ear to the Titan game broadcast. Without me there, they won. It figures.

"I guess I'm going to have to learn to like baseball," Andy said, over coffee.

"I'll take you to a game one day."

"Maybe one weekend when I have the boys," he said.

This suggestion wasn't as casual as it sounded. I had never met his two sons. He thought that it was better that they not meet me unless it looked as if we had something more lasting than a fling.

"That would be nice," I said, matching his nonchalance.

"Good, fine. We'll do it," he said.

"Just not this weekend," I laughed. "I think I'm going to be pretty busy."

"Really? How come?"

"You didn't listen to anything I told you during dinner, did you? Remember Joe Kelsey? Gay baseball player? Major scoop for your pal Kate?"

"Sorry. Of course I was listening. I just didn't connect it with this weekend. I guess I'm not all here."

"Something wrong? I've been babbling away and haven't even asked how your case is going."

"I'm still trying to tie these kids together somehow, and I can't make it fit."

"Tell me about them."

"It's not worth it. We keep going over it."

"Come on. Here's my ear. Take advantage of it."

"Why not?" he sighed. "Victim one: Benjamin Goldman. That's the one your friend was talking about. Ten years old. The youngest of three. The father is a dentist with offices at Bloor and Avenue Road."

"Serious money."

"Pots of it. The Goldmans live in a big house on Burton Road, one of those old stone mansions. The mother doesn't work. She's active in some high-profile charities. Aside from that, as far as I can see, she lunches. The older kids go to Upper Canada College. Ben was scheduled to start next year.

"He was an average student, with average interests for a kid of his class. In other words, he was a busy kid. He played hockey. He was big for his age and the star of his team. He took guitar lessons, went to religious classes, played tennis, hung around with his buddies playing video games. He wore designer clothes, had his own phone and unlimited spending money."

"Spoiled silly."

"I guess. He was last seen on a Saturday afternoon in early March on Queen Street. He had gone to a movie with a couple of friends at the Eaton Centre. They left him there – they were taking the streetcar and he was going on the subway. Then he disappeared. It was about four-thirty."

"When did his parents miss him?"

"They were out that day, too. When they got home about eight, he wasn't there. There's a maid, but she didn't know what to do when he didn't show up.

"The Goldmans called the family of the kids he'd been with, but they were out, too. They'd met the boys at their grandparents for dinner. The Goldmans didn't reach them until nine or so. Then they phoned us.

"The body turned up Monday. It had been put in a dumpster behind a plumbing supply store on Danforth Road. It's a pretty deserted place on Sundays. One of the sales clerks found him when he went to throw out some packing crates."

"Nice way to start the week. It's lucky he looked. Was the body just there, or was it in a bag or something?"

"It was wrapped in a tarp, but he saw the foot sticking out. The body was naked."

"He'd been raped, you said?"

"Well, semen was found in his anus, but it's probable that the assault happened after he died."

"You told me he was smothered."

"The killer put a plastic bag over his head. He was probably unconscious at the time. There was a sedative in his blood. A mild tranquillizer, actually."

"When did he die?"

"The coroner thinks it was probably late Saturday night."

"What else did he find?"

"He'd had a hamburger, fries, and a shake some hours before his death. He didn't have one with his friends."

"And he wasn't on tranquillizers for a legitimate reason? Or could have taken them for kicks? His mother sounds like the type that would have a medicine chest full of them."

"Maybe. You're right about the mother, but she swears that she keeps careful track of all their medications."

"What about the second victim? The boy from Regent Park."

"Maurice LeBlanc. He wasn't so little. He was twelve, and well into puberty. He died during the March school break. His mother works in the kitchen at Sick Kids' Hospital, so Maurice was on his own.

"We don't know very much about his last day. It was a Tuesday. He went to the laundromat in the morning, and bought some stuff at the convenience store at Gerrard and Sackville on his way home. He was seen getting on the westbound Carlton car at one-thirty, then zippo."

"What about the rest of the family?"

"His father's in jail for bank robbery. He's from Quebec, the mother's from Jamaica. There are no brothers and sisters."

"Family friends? Uncles?"

"We've looked into that. Nothing, so far."

"What kind of a kid was he?"

"A good kid. Everyone says so. He was an A student, a boy scout, active in a church youth group, was on the school track and field team.

"He also did babysitting around the project to help his mother out. Every mother we talked to said how trustworthy he was. He was very mature for his age, and very responsible."

"He'd have to be, I guess. How sad for his mother. Husband in jail, only child dead."

"She said that Maurice was all of her future. Now she says her hopes are gone. A nice woman."

"That just breaks my heart."

"The body wasn't found for three days. It had

been dumped off the path by the ravine by Moore Park. The weather was terrible that week. Friday morning a birder was out looking for early migrants with his dog. The dog found the body. And he wasn't the first animal that did, either."

"Oh, God."

"The coroner found the same sedative in his system and the cause of the death was the same – he was smothered with a plastic bag."

"And the latest little boy?"

"James Liu. He was eleven. The middle child of three. His parents are immigrants from China and run a restaurant in Scarborough. They both work there. The grandmother looks after the children. She lives in the house with them."

Andy got up from the couch and began to pace.

"The boy was strictly controlled, unlike the other two. He worked hard at school and helped in the restaurant. He also took violin lessons. His passion was swimming. He was a very talented kid, with a lot of potential. His coach had to work hard to convince the parents that they should let him compete. They gave in on condition that he kept his straight A average at school. He was on the way back from the swim club when he disappeared."

"And then?"

"They found him late the next night in an abandoned warehouse over by the Ex. Naked. Raped. The same stomach contents, the same semen type, but this one was raped before he died, and he was carved up a bit after he was smothered."

"Carved?"

"You don't want to know," Andy said.

"So the guy is getting more violent?"

"And more confident, I think. The pattern is changing."

"This one is really getting to you."

He rubbed his eyes, then ran his hands through his hair.

"I've got to get this guy, Kate, and soon."

"You're tired. Let's get to bed."

He took my hand and pulled me gently from the couch.

"Let's make something nice. I've had enough ugliness in the last couple of days."

So we did.

CHAPTER

12

It was still dark when I woke up. I was alone in bed, but I could hear noises in the kitchen. I grabbed my robe and staggered towards the smell of coffee and the sound of the can-opener. When I got there, Andy was feeding Elwy, out of self-defence.

"What's the matter?"

"Nothing," he said. "I woke up and decided it was a good morning for a walk. Want to come?"

"At six o'clock in the morning?"

"I'm going to see if anything interesting flew in overnight."

I knew Andy was a bird watcher. I even went out with him one afternoon on a wintry prowl through some woods north of the city, looking for owls. Other than that, during the one winter we'd been together, bird watching had consisted of standing at the kitchen window and watching the sparrows and blue jays in my feeder. I suspect that I'll learn all sorts of other strange things about him as spring progresses.

I took a cup of coffee while I considered his proposition.

"I'm leaving in ten minutes," he said.

What the hell. I went to put on some warm clothes. When I got back, Andy frowned at my sneakers.

"You need better walking shoes than that," he said.

"They're the best I've got," I grumbled, deciding the outing was a bad idea after all. I poured another cup of coffee for the road. Andy drove.

As we headed down Pottery Road towards the Bayview extension, I was glad I'd come. In the early light the willows along the road were golden with buds. There was very little traffic.

"I haven't seen the dawn for years," I said. "At least not from this end."

"If you're going to become a birder, you'll get used to it," Andy said, then reached across and squeezed my hand. I hoped he couldn't see the horror in my face. I took another swallow of coffee.

We parked the car, then headed down the path, which was slippery with mud from overnight rain. It was cold, despite the sun peeking through the haze. I looked around at the bare trees.

"No birds. Can we go home now?"

"Well, I certainly hear the call of the female grouse," Andy said, taking my hand and leading me further down the path. After another few yards he stopped and scanned the trees with his binoculars.

"Wasn't one of the bodies found in here?" I asked, shivering.

"A little further in, near the bridge. Look, up in that maple. It's a ruby-crowned kinglet."

"Where?" I peered through my binoculars. There were four leafless trees in the general vicinity of where he was pointing. Who knew which one was the maple?

"In the second tree, see the crotch where the branch heads off at about two o'clock? It's just about halfway along, on the small branch above. Sort of flipping around."

Just as I got the little bugger in my sights, it flew away.

"Nice," I said.

"Did you get it?"

"It had wings," I said.

"You just need practice," he said. "You'll get better at spotting them. Come on. I'll see if I can find you another one."

"Goody," I said, following him down the path.

"Look it up in Peterson so you know what you're after."

I dragged the field guide he'd given me for my birthday (so romantic!) out of my bag. I was looking up the damned bird when he stopped again. I bumped into him.

"Here's an easy one. That's a robin's song. Everyone knows what a robin looks like. See if you can find him. He's big."

"I don't even know where to look. Does he like the trees or the ground?"

"Yes."

"Thanks a lot."

"Listen. Follow your ears. Where does it sound like it's coming from?"

"Off to the right a bit, professor."

"High or low?"

"I can't tell."

"Try high."

I put my binoculars up and pointed them in the general direction of the sound. All I saw was a blur. When I focused, all I saw was a tree trunk.

"I can't," I said.

"Find it with your naked eye first, then focus tight."

He pointed. I saw the robin, then found it in the binoculars. I felt quite proud.

"All right," I said. "I'm ready for the hard stuff."

"That's my girl," he said, taking my hand and leading me down the path. I cringed. I don't much like being called a girl, even affectionately, but it wasn't worth fighting about. He meant well.

He didn't notice the cringe. He was too busy enjoying the birds. To tell the truth, I was even getting into it a bit. I even saw the kinglet. Cute little thing.

After a few minutes we got to the concrete pillars of the Heath Street walking bridge. There were no traces of the body that had been dumped there, but there was an evil feeling in the place. Or my imagination was working too hard. I shivered.

"Where was the body?" I asked. Andy pointed to a spot well off the path to the right. I could see remnants of the yellow crime-site ribbons in the bushes.

"We think he dumped it off the bridge."

I looked through the binoculars at the spot. Something had caught my eye, something shiny. I couldn't make out what it was.

"There's something there, Andy." I stepped off the path into the brush.

"Don't waste your time looking for clues. Our people spent two days here."

He was right. All that was there was garbage: a pop can, styrofoam junk from a fast food joint, a bright yellow film wrapper, the advertising supplement for the Eaton's Boxing Day sales – all slightly grungy from a winter under the snow.

"Litterbugs," I laughed, fighting my way back through the tangle of budding branches.

"Was there snow on the ground when the body was found?"

"Just patches," Andy said.

"It gives me the creeps to think of him carrying the body right by people's houses. How could he be sure someone wasn't watching?"

"He probably waited until the middle of the night. They would have been asleep."

"Are you going to get him?"

"Yes. There's no question in my mind. I'll never give up on this one. I just want to get him before he does it again."

"How much time do you figure you've got?"

"It's hard to know. He hasn't kept to any discernible schedule so far. I mean, he hasn't always done it on weekends, or Tuesdays, or the full moon, or some other goddamned thing. It's all so random. That's what makes it so hard."

"Is this the worst murder you've ever investigated?"

"They're all bad," he said. "They're all the worst, at the time. But other ones, no matter how brutal, have at least made some sort of twisted sense."

He stared silently at the spot where the body had lain.

"I mean that, in other cases, the victims had – quotes – done something to deserve being killed. Cheated on a violent husband, ripped off an associate in a drug deal, even been the wrong colour for some twisted racist. But not these kids. They are innocent victims. There is no sense to these killings."

"Not one we know, anyway."

How could there be?" he snapped at me. "I don't even believe in God, but this man is the son of Satan. This man is evil. I have to stop him."

He stopped talking, abruptly. Neither of us moved for a minute or so. Then we heard a strange, tootling noise. Andy laughed.

"Sorry about that. I guess I'm being a little bit melodramatic. Let's go find that blue jay."

"Is that what that sound is?"

"Yeah, he's courting. You've got to see this."

We went further down the path, towards the sound. Suddenly, he stopped and pointed.

"There he is – nine o'clock in the tree right ahead."

I found the bird in my binoculars, and began to laugh. He was doing little pliés on the branch, bobbing up and down in time to the toodeloo sounds.

"That's supposed to turn some lady blue jay on?" I laughed. "They've got strange tastes."

"It's irresistible," Andy said.

"Try me," I said.

He stuck his elbows out and bobbed up and down like the blue jay, his head to one side, quizzically.

"Wanta screw? Wanta screw?"

"Not with you. You're out of your mind."

We spent an hour in the ravine. It was a nice escape. Peaceful, even. And we still made it home before the time I usually woke up.

Andy got the first shower while I started breakfast. I put Elwy out into the garden so he wouldn't steal bacon. By the time Andy had used up all the hot water, the table was set. We sat down to eggs, bacon, and fried tomatoes, each with a section of the paper, probably the only couple in the city in which the woman gets the sports section first. The phone rang as I started reading the box scores. That early, I didn't think it was for me.

I was right. When Andy got off the phone, he was all business.

"There's a letter for me that might be from the killer. I have to go."

While he was dressing, I stuck an egg and a couple of pieces of bacon between two slices of toast.

"Don't drip it on your tie," I said. He gave me a quick kiss.

"See you later. There's a party I have to go to for one of the homicide secretaries. She's going on maternity leave."

"That's sweet."

"Want to come?"

"Maybe. Call me later."

"Will do."

Elwy dashed in the open door when Andy left. We discussed the events of the day while I did the dishes.

"I don't know, Fatso, things are getting interesting here. First he wants me to meet his kids. Now he's letting loose with his colleagues."

Andy and I had never gone out with his friends before. Partly for the same reason he'd kept me from his kids, I guess. But there was another reason, too. It went back to the Titan murders last fall. Since I had figured out the identity of the killer before Andy did, and because of what I do for a living, there had been a certain amount of ink about my detecting. This had caused Andy some grief around the shop. He had come to terms with being beaten by an amateur, but some of his colleagues still resented it, thinking it had reflected badly on the homicide squad. Threatened their manhood or something. And homicide cops are as macho as they come.

I decided to get in to work early so I could be finished in time to mingle with the boys in blue. I also paid a little more attention than usual to my clothes. Usually on days when I'm not going to be out of the office I settle for jeans and a sweatshirt. This time I decided on one of my more elegant reporter disguises, a soft green jersey dress with quarterback shoulder pads that shows off my eyes and makes my waist look tiny.

Why not? I might as well try to make an impression. Elwy told me I looked just fine. I gave him a handful of catnip.

"Go crazy, chum," I said.

CHAPTER

13

"This is the sports department, boys and girls. Please be quiet so the reporters can do their work."

I turned in my chair and checked out the dozen or so kids standing three feet behind my desk. Most of them were managing to contain their excitement at being at the very epicentre of journalistic excellence. The guide, a woman from the paper's public-relations department who was dressed in a suit that probably cost more than my entire wardrobe, could barely stifle her yawns. The kids were poking each other and making rude remarks behind their hands. T.C. smiled at me from the back of the pack.

"Let them talk," I said. "I'd like to hear what they think of the paper. You, the young man with the glasses. You look like an intelligent sort. Who do you think is the best sportswriter in Toronto?"

"Well, that's a tough question, Ma'am. I think I'll have to go with Katherine Henry."

"What is it about her work you find so compelling?"

"Well, I guess it's because you are my mum's best friend and our landlady, too."

That got their interest. Some of them began to giggle. I laughed with them.

"And here I thought you admired me for my talents alone. Listen, do you have any questions about sports reporting? I'd be glad to answer them."

It took a moment for the first one to get the courage to raise her hand, but once they started, the kids lost their shyness. An impromptu seminar on sports and journalism followed, ranging in subject from computers to headlines to photographs and the inevitable questions about what the athletes are really like.

My colleagues, at first annoyed by the chatter, soon caught the enthusiasm. Some of them had questions of their own.

"How many of you read the school sports reports?" asked Dickie Greaves. Most of the hands shot into the air.

"What do you think?"

"It's really neat to see people you know in the paper," said one girl.

"You should have more pictures," said another.

"You haven't done our baseball team yet," complained T.C. "We were champions last year, too."

"What position do you play?"

"Pitcher."

"He's good, too," said the boy next to him, his best friend, Larry. "He almost pitched a no-hitter last year."

"Well, I can't be everywhere," Dickie said. "You have to let me know about these things. What's your team called?"

"Riverdale Rogues," T.C. said.

Dickie made a large show of making a note. What a grandstander!

"Let me know when you're playing and I'll come out sometime," he said.

"All right!"

The chorus of approval was accompanied by a few high fives. When the commotion had ended, Ms. P.R. decided it was time to take back control.

"Boys and girls, we have to move on to the composing room now. We've taken up too much of the nice lady's time."

Grumbling, the group moved on, but not before shaking hands all around.

"What is that 'boys and girls' shit?" Dickie asked. "Why do people think they have to condescend to children like that? They're not idiots, just young."

"You were great with them," I said. "I never realized what a star you are."

"Well, I write about what they care about. I have a big readership. Something that some people around here don't seem to realize."

"Point taken, Dickie," said Jake Watson, who had come out of his office to see what the fuss was about. "Wasn't that T.C. with the group?"

"Yeah," I said.

"He's shot up since I last saw him."

"Three inches since Christmas. Sally's going nuts trying to keep him in clothes. But he's ecstatic.

No one calls him Shrimp any more."

"He's a nice kid," Dickie said. "Are you really close?"

"Close as we can be without being related," I said. "I adore him. Thanks for being so nice to him. I'm sure it made him feel special. And if you don't follow through on that story you promised, I'll be the one who gets the heat."

"All right, Kate," Jake said. "If you're through assigning features, I'd like a word."

We went down to the cafeteria for coffee, settling ourselves in the tiny smoking section behind a recently erected partition. In this corner of the room, there was no attempt to match the fern-bar décor of the main dining room. I guess the building management thinks that smokers don't deserve amenities.

"How's the Kelsey piece going?"

"Not bad. I should be finished by this afternoon. Have we got the photos?"

"Of Joe," Jake said. "He and his friend decided not to have any taken together. Sandy figured it was enough for Joe to declare himself without putting a face to his lover."

"Also, he's got his own career in San Francisco. I don't think he hides the fact that he's gay, but he doesn't need to hit the tabloids. It's a private matter."

"You're probably right. I just hope that Joe doesn't chicken out."

"It's his right, Jake. But I don't think he will. Where is it running?"

"I fought to keep in the sports section, so I can give it bigger play. You have to write a short front-page piece pointing to it, but you can have as much space as you want inside."

"I can spin it out as long as you like, but after I've said the obvious, there's not a lot to say."

"I'd like to give you a full page. We'll fill some of that with art, of course, but can you give us fifty, fifty-five inches?"

"I'll do my best. I feel like I'm going to have to run some of this by Joe. That's not something I usually do, but I think these are special circumstances."

"Okay, do what you think is right. I trust your judgement."

"Shucks, boss, thanks a lot. I'll call him this afternoon, when I'm done."

"Better call earlier and check what time he leaves for the ballpark. I'd like the go-ahead before the end of the day so we can get the piece ready for Saturday."

"You're right again. I'll call him as soon as I get upstairs."

"Thanks."

Joe agreed to take a look at the piece as long as I got to his place before 4:00, so I worked through lunch and had a semi-final draft done on time. I drove to his condo on Front Street by the market. A security guard with a skimpy moustache and traces of acne interrogated me intensely before getting on the phone to Joe.

Why is it that giving people uniforms automatically turns them into assholes? And what kind of question is that from a woman in love with a cop?

Grudgingly, Mr. Law and Order told me to proceed to the fifth floor, corner suite, which turned out to look remarkably like any boring rental unit, despite its hefty price tag. A one-bedroom in this joint was worth more than half a mil, but Joe's place, with its off-white walls, beige furnishings, and hotel-room art, didn't look it.

They were both waiting for me. I handed the printout to Joe while Sandy fetched coffee. Joe leafed through the story slowly, handing Sandy each page as he finished.

"Well? What's the verdict?"

"You can really write," Sandy said, sounding surprised.

"It is how I make my living," I said, bristling, but I was pleased by the compliment. "So much for style. What about content? Is there anything there that gives you problems? Have I got the facts straight?"

"I didn't think you'd put that in about Sultan blackmailing me," Joe said.

"It's an interesting footnote to the killings, and it's key to you making your decision, right? What about the rest of it? Have I got your background right – all the biographical stuff?"

"Yes, there aren't any mistakes. It just makes me uncomfortable, seeing it all spelled out like this. The way it's going to look."

"I never pretended it was going to be easy, Joe. Are you having second thoughts about going through with it?"

"No. When is this coming out?"

"Saturday. Day after tomorrow."

"I guess I'd better make a few calls."

"Who to?" Sandy asked. I wondered, too. Not anyone who was in a position to scoop me, I hoped.

"My mom, for one. My brother."

"Well, yes. I imagine the story will get on the wire pretty quickly. Better she hear it from you. I'd just rather you didn't tell anyone in Toronto. I mean none of the press. Presumably you're going to want to tell some of your team-mates, but I'd really like to get the exclusive. I know that sounds kind of insensitive, but if you could wait, say, until after the press has left tomorrow night, I'd appreciate it."

"I just want to tell Eddie and Tiny, maybe Gloves."

"Whatever you like."

"It will probably be easier just to let the rest find out from the newspaper, really," said Sandy. "Easier for you, anyway. What about your manager?"

"Or the owner," I said. "Do you think maybe Ted Ferguson should know?"

"I don't know how I could tell the skipper something like this. He's going to be real mad."

"What about one of the coaches? Maybe you could tell Sugar."

Sugar Jenkins, the batting coach, is about as sensitive as they get in this business. Which doesn't quite make him Alan Alda, but he's not Clint Eastwood, either.

"And he could tell Red," Sandy said.

"Maybe. I'm getting pretty nervous about this."

"Joe and I have been talking about how he's going to handle all the media coverage, Kate," Sandy said. "Have you got any suggestions?"

"Well, it's going to be pretty overwhelming," I said. "I expect that there are going to be people coming in from all over the place. *Sports Illustrated*,

Sporting News, the big networks from both countries, the sports channels, gay publications. Ted Koppel, for God's sake. For a guy as quiet as you, that's going to be hard to handle. Maybe you could set up some sort of ground rules."

"Like what?"

"You could give a press conference about your sexuality, then stop talking about it. Or you could have Hugh Marsh set up interviews off the field. Oh, Jesus. Marsh. He's going to be freaked."

"I wish I could just talk to you and get it over with."

"It's not that easy. But you have every right to carve yourself out some privacy. I think you would be happier if you just talked baseball when you're at the ballpark. I don't know why reporters wouldn't respect that. If you stick to it, they won't have any choice. Then you can decide what other interviews you're going to do."

"Maybe one press conference just to confirm the story, Joe," said Sandy. "Then you can do what Kate suggests. It's all spelled out here in the story, anyway."

"It all depends upon how much of a symbol you want to become. It's up to you. There will be no shortage of people to talk to. You'll hit the big time. Johnny Carson. Oprah, even. It's your choice."

"I'm not doing this for the publicity," Joe said. "I'm doing it because I have to, but then I want to forget about it."

"The best thing you can do is keep on playing as well as you have been and not show that the attention is getting to you," I said. "That's going to shut up a lot of the criticism, anyway. Is that going to be a problem?"

"I can't tell now, but I feel like making this decision has taken all the pressure off me. I feel great. But I don't know what I'll feel like after."

"I'll be here," Sandy said.

"You know if you want to talk about it, I will too," I said. I don't usually form friendships with ballplayers, but Joe's case was special.

"What will be, will be," said Joe, standing up. "I'd better get to the ballpark."

"I gathered up my things and headed for the door.

"I won't be around tonight or tomorrow, Joe," I said, "but I'll be there early on Saturday."

"Oh, yes, you'll want to enjoy that scoop, won't you," he said, smiling.

"And you know it," I laughed.

CHAPTER

14

I stood in a corner at the cop shop party, surrounded by noise and strangers, watching Andy make his way through the crowd to the impromptu bar set up in one of the glass-walled interview rooms. He was stopped several times along the way, usually by women.

I love watching him, especially when he doesn't know it. Just looking at him arouses me. After spending six years with the same man, I had forgotten about the lustful yearning that goes with the beginning of an affair, but it's nice to find it again in what is popularly considered creaking middle-age.

The party wasn't bad. One of the advantages of being a baseball writer is that it's never difficult to get a conversation going with strangers, especially men. Most of them think a woman sportswriter is a bit like a roller-skating duck, so amazed are they that something in a skirt knows more about jock stuff than they do, which gives an interesting edge to the conversation.

The more macho types try, and fail, to dazzle me with sports trivia. Then there are the men, and I have known some of them rather well, for whom I am a fantasy come true: a woman they can go to bed with and talk baseball afterwards.

My reveries were interrupted by a beefy guy who might as well have had "cop" tattooed on his forehead. He had a closely trimmed moustache and piggy little close-set eyes. Some would call him handsome, himself included, I'm sure, but he looked too mean for my taste. He was dressed in an expensive sports jacket which strained slightly at the seams, and he had a smirk on his face.

"Well, well, if it isn't the lady-reporter hotshot detective. Are you here to solve our latest murders for us?"

This guy had obviously been to the Academy of Snappy Opening Lines. I decided to duck the hostility with as much charm as I could muster.

"I'm just here as a guest of Staff Sergeant Munro. Your new offices are very nice. You must be pleased with them."

"Pretty sexy stuff, eh? Not like the hole we used to work in."

The homicide department had just moved into the new post-modern police headquarters on College Street, an amazing edifice of polished red granite and blue steel that looked as if it should house the head office of Canada's Wonderland or McDonald's, not Serve and Protect, Inc. Inside, it was all computer-sleek and tasteful.

The homicide department on the third floor had no sense of drama or importance. It was just a medium-sized room furnished with modern, slick work-cubicles, so anonymous and lacking in character that it might as well have been an insurance office. The only signs of the deadly and dangerous nature of the business conducted here were cardboard boxes full of files piled in the corners, with the names of notorious crimes scrawled on them in black magic-marker.

"Yes, you must be glad to have moved," I said, looking for Andy over the guy's shoulder. He edged closer, slopping the drink in his little plastic glass.

"But you're not here for the décor. You've got a thing for cops now, don't you? What's the matter, get tired of those big nigger dicks down at the ballpark?"

It's not often that I'm at a loss for words, but all I could do was try to keep my jaw from dropping. He went on.

"But if you're looking for action, what are you doing with that faggot Munro? You look like you could use some of my kind of loving. I bet you like a little of the rough stuff. Slow and hard and rough. How about it?"

I could feel my face turning red.

"Excuse me," I said and began to move away, but he had his hands on the wall on either side of me. I was considering the etiquette of a knee to the groin in this particular social situation when Andy arrived.

"I see you've met Sergeant Flanagan," he said. The beefy cop stepped back and Andy handed me my glass.

"We hadn't exchanged names," I said.

"Bob and I joined the force at the same time," Andy said, putting his arm over the lout's shoulder. "We've followed in each other's footsteps ever since. How's it going, pal?"

"Can't complain, Andy. Nice little lady you've got here. I was just telling her what a lucky guy you are."

With a hearty-guy slap on the back, he was gone.

"Who is that scumbucket?"

"Oh, he's not so bad. Just a bit rough around the edges. He's a good cop."

"He's not much of a human being," I said. "He was coming on to me."

"That just shows he's got good taste," Andy said, kissing me on the cheek. "Look, finish your drink. We're going out to dinner with Jim Wells and his wife."

He gulped what was left in his glass and waved Jim Wells, his partner, in our direction. He came right over with a pleasant-looking woman in tow.

"Kate, you know Jim, but I don't think you've met Carol," he said. "I'm just going to say goodbye to Lorna and we'll be on our way."

Seething, I made small talk with the Wellses while Andy went to embrace a hugely pregnant woman with a rock-star mane of curls. Despite her shape, she was wearing a mini-skirt and patterned stockings. Flanagan joined them, fondled her belly, and said something that made them all roar with laughter. Andy was still smiling when he came back.

"Where to, folks? Anyone feel like Greek food? We can head into Kate's neighbourhood, then back to her place for a drink afterward."

I couldn't believe what I was hearing. First, he buddies up with some pig who has just been speaking filth to me. Then he makes dinner arrangements with his partner without consulting me. Now he volunteers my home for his party.

"Sounds great," Wells said. "Me for some souvlaki."

I didn't trust myself to speak. Andy put his arm around me when we got outside. I imitated a block of ice. Jim and Carol were at the curb, waiting to hail a cab.

"What's the matter?" asked Mr. Perceptive.

"I don't want to talk about it," I hissed.

"What did I do?"

"Nothing. Forget it. There's no problem. Look, they've got a cab."

I chattered on the way over, determined not to let my mood show. I'm middle-class enough to loathe fighting in public. I must have been convincing. Andy soon relaxed.

We got out of the cab at the Carrot Common, the health-food mall, complete with yoga centre, organic butcher, and New Age crystal store.

"I've heard of this place," Carol said. "It's supposed to be really great."

I took her on a tour of the windows of the closed stores. We both gawked at the kids' clothes arrayed to tempt double-income parents looking to make a status statement through their toddlers. There was a sale on. A sleeper for a six-month-old, in tie-dyed black, was reduced to a mere $65.

"Regularly ninety-four," I pointed out.

"I'll take a dozen," Carol said. I was beginning to like her.

Jim and Andy were waiting for us in front of the crystal store.

"I don't get it," Jim said. "This store is full of rocks. They're kind of pretty, but what are they for?"

"Channelling," I said. "Getting in touch with past selves or higher truth or something like that. It's hocus-pocus, just like when we were hippies, but we didn't go in for the high-priced accessories."

"I was never a hippie," Jim said.

"Of course not," I said.

There was the usual lineup at the Astoria and it wasn't warm enough for the Omonia terrace to be open yet, so we went to the unfashionable south side of the Danforth where the food is just as good and you don't have to wait for it.

We ordered a bottle of retsina and settled in with the menus.

"I saw you talking to God's gift to sex-starved women, Kate," Carol said. "Did Bob Flanagan pour on his famous charm?"

"Hardly," I said. "What's that guy's story, anyway?"

"It's not a nice one," Jim said. "He was a good cop, but can't control his temper. He beat up a suspect last year – an innocent suspect as it turned out – and got suspended. Now he's back on the force, but he's doing community relations work. He can't stand it."

"He's getting into the booze, too," Andy said.

"Community relations? That boor?" I said, amazed. "What do they have him doing, talking to battered women's groups?"

"Worse," Jim said. "He's doing school assemblies with Honker the talking Police Car."

Carol snickered, and I joined her.

"Okay, it's funny," Andy conceded. "But it's killing Bob. And he is a good cop."

"What was he doing at the party tonight if he's not at homicide any more?"

"He can't stay away, I guess," Jim said. "He hangs around whenever he's off duty. And Lorna wanted him there. They're buddies."

The harried waitress arrived to take our orders. When she left, the men changed the subject.

"Did you go and talk to that guy at U of T this afternoon?" asked Jim.

"Harold Josephson, yes. He didn't have much new."

"Who's he?" I asked.

"A psychology prof. He's doing a study on mass and serial murder," Jim explained.

"It was a pretty useless conversation," he continued. "If our guy is a true serial killer, we're going to have to wait for him to slip up or hope for some incredible piece of luck."

"Why is that?" Carol asked.

"Because serial killers tend to hit at random," Andy said. "It's a crime without a motive, except in the mind of the killer. There's no previous connection between them and the victims. So digging around in the kids' histories isn't going to help. Neither is looking for a connection among them. The connection is only in the killer's mind."

"What did he say about the letter?" asked Jim.

"He thinks it's the real thing, too."

"Is that the one that came in this morning? What did it say?"

Andy shot me a quick warning look.

"You know better than to ask me that."

Yeah, fuck off and die to you, too. Andy returned his attention to his trusted colleague.

"It might be a break. It means that he's reaching out, looking for attention."

"We can hope. But didn't Josephson tell you that these guys are smarter than the average crook?"

"Yes, but we're smarter than the average cops."

The two exchanged smiles and clinked glasses.

"I read an article about serial killers once," Carol said. "They seem to have quite a few things in common. Isn't there some sort of psychological profile you can work up?"

"That's why I spent three hours with Josephson this afternoon. There are some behaviour patterns that have emerged through the study of people like Ted Bundy or John Wayne Gacy, who killed all those boys in Chicago, but they aren't obvious. One of the frustrating things about serial killers is that many of them are apparently completely normal. It's only after they have been caught that we find out that they fit the profile."

"Bundy was charming."

"Right," her husband agreed. "He was so damn normal no one suspected him. That's the bitch of it."

"What about the child molesters?" Carol asked. "Do serial killers usually start their careers with other types of crime?"

"Our guy might or might not have a record," Andy said. "But I would bet he hasn't. This son-of-a-bitch is not going to make our lives any easier by wandering around schoolyards, foaming at the mouth and offering little boys candy. That's why it's so goddamned frustrating."

He stared gloomily at his wine before sloshing it down in one gulp. He refilled his glass without noticing anyone else's. Carol Wells leaned across the table in the sudden morose silence and touched my hand.

"Get used to it, Kate. You are seeing what happens to ordinarily sweet human beings when they are in the middle of a case. Don't take it personally."

That got the men's attention. They exchanged a giance, then laughed.

"Right, we're not on duty now," Jim said, filling the other glasses at the table. "Let's talk about something pleasant."

CHAPTER

15

Once we had changed the topic of conversation, the evening improved. We talked about trips we had taken, about journalism, about the Wells's kids. It was past 11:00 when we left the restaurant and pleasant enough outside to stroll the Danforth, checking out the gift shop windows full of the kind of horrid, tacky statuary that must clutter up the apartments of half the Greek newlyweds in town. These shops are a reassuring counterpoint to the gentrification of the neighbourhood, cheek by jowl with the new, trendier, stores. Jim and Carol turned down the invitation, mine this time, to come back for coffee or a drink.

We were close to Allen's when we saw them into a cab, so Andy and I went in and got a booth. While Andy ordered armagnacs for us both at the bar, I picked out some of my favourites on the vintage jukebox. There's a choice at Allen's – old jazz or old rhythm-and-blues. I selected the quieter numbers from both genres, an attempt to pre-empt the tastes of a rowdy group at the bar that looked like a soft-ball team that had mistaken the place for the sports bar down the street. Wouldn't they be surprised when their bar bill arrived. Max, the owner, sat at the corner of the bar, the silver star imbedded in his right front tooth glinting when he smiled at the willowy society sweetie fawning over him. He was wearing his purple-framed round glasses and looked like a decadent little owl.

"All right, tell me about the note," I said. "That is, if I'm allowed to have that information."

"Stop being a jerk. What I tell you is confidential. I just want to keep it that way. I am breaking the rules by talking to an outsider. Jim may be my partner, but he's still a cop. I look bad."

"Don't be ridiculous. You don't think that Jim tells Carol everything?"

"As a matter of fact, I don't. She's not interested. Most women aren't as nosy as you are."

"Oh, nosy, am I? I prefer to say that I'm inquisitive. That's my job."

"No. Your job is only to be inquisitive about overpaid morons and the games they play."

"Fine. Don't tell me, then. I thought you liked talking about your cases with me."

We sat in hostile silence for a few minutes, avoiding each other's eyes, waiting each other out. Andy finally spoke.

"All right. I'll show it to you. It was pretty strange. It was faxed to me."

"Oh, great, a high-tech wacko. A yuppie serial killer. Do you suppose he sent it on his car phone?"

"Here's a copy."

He passed a folded sheet of paper across the table. I opened it. At first it looked just funny, a kid's joke cut out of magazines and newspapers. It was well-designed, a collage of headlines about the crimes, photographs of the crime scenes, underlined paragraphs cut from the reports. But the words were chilling: "How are you doing, Munro? Not so good? Too bad. You haven't got much time. I have my next victim chosen. The stalking has begun."

"Catch me if you can," I said.

"That's about it. This is not unusual for a serial killer. The demand for attention, and the desire to be caught. In his more rational moments, this kind of guy often really wants to be stopped."

"Well, you can tell a few things about him. He's neat, for one thing. He probably got straight A's in kindergarten. Isn't there a way you can trace where a fax has come from?"

"It's not easy if the sender wants to be anonymous. We might be able to get something from Bell Canada, eventually, but it will take time."

"What else is happening?"

"Well, we're keeping a bunch of our constables busy going door to door again. Sometimes people don't realize what they've seen, or it's so trivial they don't realize how important it is. We're launching another public appeal tomorrow."

"Boring work. Is that how you usually find your killer?"

"No. It's usually someone the victim knows. Half the time we find them with the knife or gun in their hand. Even when it's not handed to us, we can focus on likely suspects. This time we can't."

"So what do you go on?"

"For example, someone on Heath Street saw a dark van on the street the night before the second kid was found in the ravine. Now we go back to all the people we talked to on the other two crimes and see if they saw a van, too. It might not have seemed worth mentioning the first time we talked to them."

"Who saw it?"

"An old guy with insomnia who looked out his window at two in the morning. It stood out for him because he knows all the cars on the street. In the mixed commercial and residential areas the other two were found in, it wouldn't be so unusual."

"So, what do you do?"

"We talk to all the neighbours on Heath Street, for a start, to find out if they had a visitor who had a van. And we talk to people like the guy in the all-night doughnut shop near the plumbing supply store where they found the first body. If any of them saw one, too, then we begin to think it might be important."

"Straws in the wind."

"You got it. We're just slogging. The traffic guys are having fun interviewing anybody who got a parking ticket in the neighbourhoods involved. It all goes in the computer, and I make myself crazy going through the printouts. I keep thinking that maybe I missed something."

"But what are you looking for?"

Who the fuck knows?" he said wearily. "I've felt all along that this one isn't going to solved by the routine stuff, but we can't be sure."

"You think this guy is smart?"

"I think that he thinks he is. I think that's why he sent me that thing."

"Don't let it get to you, Andy," I said. "Let's just forget about it for tonight."

"I can't do that, Kate. Carol was right. There comes a point in an investigation where it just takes over my life. If you're going to get involved with a cop, you're going to have to understand that."

"Andy, I didn't get involved with a cop. I got involved with a man. A wonderful man. A human being, not some sort of crime-busting robot. I want to know where he has gone."

"Oh, please. Let's can the meaningful relationship conversation for tonight. I'm tired."

"What about me? I'm tired, too. Tired of playing second fiddle to your murderer."

"That's typical," he said. "I'm sorry, Kate, but the world doesn't revolve around you."

"I understand the pressure you are under," I began.

"No you don't," he snapped. "You are not a cop. Just because you like to play detective doesn't make you any different from any other civilian."

"And maybe you're no different from any other cop. Maybe you have more in common with that scumbucket I met at the party tonight than you do with me."

"What are you talking about now?"

"That noble law-enforcer at the party who reminded me why I don't much like cops."

"Flanagan?"

"Yes, that rough-around-the-edges guy who likes talking about 'big nigger dicks.' That charmer."

"Oh, for Christ's sake, Kate. I can't believe that you're getting bent out of shape by something like that."

"The guy is a pig. He's sexist, racist, and vulgar."

I told Andy what Flanagan had said to me. He rolled his eyes and laughed.

"And you didn't belt him? I'm amazed at your self-restraint."

"I'm sorry, but I fail to find the humour in this."

"All right. Bob's not exactly subtle. But you can handle that kind of stuff. Things aren't exactly a tea party in the locker room are they?"

"Oh, now we're getting into it. I spend time with naked men, so I'm a slut, right? Just because my job puts me into that situation means I don't deserve any respect."

"I didn't say that."

"You didn't have to."

Even the bozos at the bar had noticed our raised voices. When I got up and walked towards the door, they moved silently out of my way. At the door, I turned back towards Andy.

"If you like him so much, you can just go spend the night with Flanagan."

As the door closed behind me, I heard the bozos cheer.

I walked around for half an hour before I went home, stomping off my rage. I half expected Andy to be waiting for me when I got there, and had been rehearsing the good lines I hadn't thought of while we were at the bar. But the house was dark. No Andy. No note. No message on the machine.

I felt let down, a bit stupid, and a little drunk. I

sat with my feet up on the couch to wait for him. Elwy came and sat on my lap, kneading his paws into my stomach and purring.

"What will I do, Elwy? Should I call him?"

He didn't answer.

"Meow if you think I should phone him."

Silence.

"You're probably right. We'll sleep on it, and it will be all right in the morning."

We headed into the bedroom. I got out of my party clothes, including the garter belt I had worn to surprise and titillate Andy, and into the comforting blue flannel nightie.

We curled up together under the duvet. Elwy was asleep in minutes. I was awake for half the night, worrying about Andy, worrying about my Kelsey feature, worrying about what would happen to Joe when the story appeared. And thinking about the killer out there somewhere, stalking.

CHAPTER

16

I planned to take the day off, but went into the office late in the morning to have a look at the layout of the Kelsey piece for the next morning's paper. I was glad to see that Jake had handled it with a bit of restraint, by which I mean that the headline stopped short of shrieking "PREACHER KELSEY IS A FLAMING FAG." The photos were good: Kelsey laughing with his team-mates, thoughtful in the on-deck circle, and at home, relaxed.

We were in Jake's office, still trying to keep the lid on the thing, to make sure the other papers didn't find out. The design department had been sworn to secrecy.

"I love it, Jake. It's really nice looking. What page is it running on?"

"Three, with a big pointer on the section page. Plus the small story on the front, with a picture. Can you write that before you go? We just need a short sell."

"No problem. What are we going to do on the weekend?"

"Which 'we' is that, kimosabe? You are going to be covering it like astroturf. Don't worry about the game story, just get reaction. Players, fans, whatever happens."

"You mean I have to go down in the stands and ask questions of strangers? Yuck."

"It's a tough life, Kate. But a noble profession."

The coffee trolley had rolled in. First in line was Margaret Papadakis. We smiled insincerely at each other.

"How's it going, Margaret? Still on the murders?"

"Mainly. There's not much happening. I hope I'll get some new stuff out of my lunch."

"What lunch is that?"

"Oh, I'm sorry. Perhaps I have been indiscreet. I assumed you knew that your friend Staff Sergeant Munro was taking me to lunch today."

"Oh, of course. It just slipped my mind. I think he wants to make a public appeal."

"He can appeal to this part of the public whenever he wants," she said, gliding away. I contemplated the effect that a full-tilt catfight would have in the newsroom and decided not to go for her firm young throat.

"Have fun," I said.

"Looks like Never on Sunday is after your man," murmured Dickie across the desk divider.

"No shit, Sherlock."

"You're not worried about her, are you? No one in his right mind would prefer her to you."

"Thanks, Dickie. Even if it's not true. I'm just feeling a bit insecure today."

Much to my own surprise, I found myself telling Greaves about my stupid behaviour the night before. He was very sympathetic.

"He sounds like my dad. When he was on a case, he was a different person. He was a nice guy, but when he got into the middle of an investigation, I wouldn't go near him. I was as likely as not to get slapped around for playing ball in the driveway."

"I don't think Andy would go that far."

"I don't think he would dare. I just meant that everybody has two sides to him. When people are under pressure, sometimes their personality changes."

"It's just that he gets so selfish."

"And you don't when you are on a big story?"

"No, I don't. I'm on a big story right now, and I have time for him."

This wasn't really true. The story had been handed to me. All I had to do was write it down. I thought about the busy times in my job. I sure wouldn't want to have Andy around while I was covering the World Series.

"Well, I've been wrong before. Maybe you are a rare and perfect creature after all. Would you like to run away with me to Tahiti?"

"Thanks for the offer. I think I'll call Andy and apologize instead. Thanks for the ear."

"Any time."

The phone was answered on the first ring.

"Homicide. Flanagan."

Damn.

"Staff Sergeant Munro, please."

"He's on another line. Want to leave a message?"

"I'll hold."

And hold, and hold, and hold some more. After

about five minutes, Flanagan was back on the line.

"Are you still there? He's still talking. Can someone else help you?"

"No, I don't think so."

"It looks like he's stuck. You'd better leave a message."

I left my name, hoping Flanagan wouldn't spew more filth down the phone line, but he just grunted and hung up.

Half an hour later I watched Margaret Papadakis sashay out the door. So did Dickie Greaves.

"A bunch of us are going up to Brandy's. Why don't you come along?" he said.

Why not? Even uninspired food in a fern forest was preferable to sitting and waiting for a phone that wouldn't ring. The restaurant was favoured by the male reporters because of the waitresses, chosen more for their pulchritude than their aptitude, and was always packed.

Walking up Yonge and along the Esplanade, I had to endure hockey talk. The Leafs were threatening to back into the playoffs again. By the time we had settled around a couple of tables in the middle of the room, the talk had switched to some Canadian boxer's chances in an upcoming fight. He was turning pro after winning a silver medal at the Olympics. Being a one-sport woman, I didn't have much to add to the conversation.

"The guy he's fighting is a bum," said Jack Connors, who wasn't letting his opinion of the fight stop him from accepting a trip to Las Vegas to cover it.

"They're starting him off slowly," said Jeff Glebe. "He's got to work up to a good match."

"Yeah, but he shouldn't be wasting his time with bums," Connors growled.

"So, what are his chances?" I asked. "He seems like such a nice kid."

"He is," Dickie said. "I knew him when he was really a kid. He was twelve when I wrote my first story about him."

"Right, I'd forgotten you'd worked in Timmins," Jack said. "What was he like then?"

"He was skinny, but determined," Dickie said. "I never thought he had a chance, but he's gone a long way on guts. I hope he makes it."

"Timmins, eh? That's a real hot spot," teased Harry Kobayashi, the football writer. "Lots of major sport there."

"Not exactly," Greaves said, smiling. "But hey, the junior men's figure-skating champion came from there. I got to go to Cleveland for the Worlds."

"Fag sport," said Harry and Jack, in unison. They all laughed. In the toy department, sports like figure-skating, golf, and tennis aren't considered real manly.

By the time the food and beer arrived, we had moved on to hot topics from the front section.

"What do you think about these murders, Kate?" Connors asked.

"Goddamned pervert fags," growled Harry Kobayashi. "They should all be locked up."

Oh, wasn't he going to enjoy my story on Preacher!

"Why do you assume the guy's gay?" I asked.

"Well he buggered the little boys, didn't he? That's the only thing those guys think about. Little boys."

"Neanderthal man strikes again," I said. "The killer is obviously a monster. With that kind of twisted mind, sex is just another form of violence."

"I still say the cops should back the paddy wagon up to all the gay bars and get them off the street," Harry said. "That would stop the killings in a hurry."

"I think Kate's right," said Greaves. "The guy isn't necessarily gay."

"What the fuck do you know about it?"

"Well, I knew one of the victims, you know."

"Big fucking deal."

"That's why I'm so interested in the case," Dickie continued.

"And here I thought you just got your jollies from death," Harry said.

"Really, it's a fascinating case," Dickie said. "Don't you agree, Kate?"

"Horrifying is more the word I would use," I said. "Maybe grotesque."

"I try to get inside the killer's head," Dickie said, taking a bite out of his hamburger. "What would make someone kill these children? Why the way he does it? Why does he smother them, instead of shoot them, or stab them? There's something almost gentle about the way he does it."

"Come on, guys, let's change the subject," said Jeff Glebe. "You're putting me off my lunch."

Not obviously. Jeff had stowed away two appetizers and was working on an entree. And was still skinny as a pencil.

"Well, I just hope they catch the guy," Dickie said.

116

"I think they will," I said, loyal to that rat, Munro. "I know they will. It's just a matter of time. But time is something they haven't got a lot of."

"He usually takes a couple of weeks between victims, doesn't he?" Jack asked.

"The pattern has been changing, though," said Greaves. "There was a month between the first two, then three weeks before the third."

"And the murders got more brutal," Jeff said. "It looks like the guy is getting pretty sure of himself."

"I'll tell you one thing. If I had a kid, I wouldn't let him out of my sight," I said.

"I guess most parents feel that way, but it's impossible," Jack said. "They have to go to school. They go to play sports, they have music lessons. How are you going to protect them, short of keeping them home all day?"

"Besides, this killer is smart," Greaves said. "He'll find a way."

On this gloomy note, I threw a twenty on the table.

"I'll let you guys carry on," I said. "I'm going to see what I can salvage of my afternoon off."

"See you at the game tomorrow," Jeff said.

"Be ready for a busy day," I said. "There might be more going on than you think."

I picked up the Citroën at the *Planet* parking lot and slid back the cloth roof. It was finally, or at least momentarily, real spring weather.

I went up the Bayview extension to the ballet studio at which I take class sporadically. I was a serious student when I was younger, with dreams of joining the National Ballet. But puberty took care of that. No matter what my talent might have been, there's not much demand for prima ballerinas who are five foot nine, with tits.

But I still enjoy putting my body through the familiar routines. It beats jogging as a way to fight the ravages of age, late nights, and too many cigarettes. I have a barre in my study, and make it to class whenever I can. Madame was one of my teachers when I was a kid. She gets furious when too much time goes by between visits, but has come to accept that I'll never be a regular. She lets me join whatever class is going.

That afternoon it was an early afternoon beginners' class for housewives. I worked up a good sweat and felt like a swan among pigeons.

When I got home I called the office to check for messages. Andy hadn't called. Throwing the last of my pride away, I phoned him. Bob Flanagan answered again, and was it my imagination, or was he pleased to tell me that Andy hadn't come back from lunch yet? It was 3:30 in the afternoon.

"The hell with him, Elwy," I said. "Let's go dig in the garden."

CHAPTER

17

The space in the backyard not taken up by the old brick garage wasn't really big enough to be called a garden, but I did my best. That's the trade-off for living close to downtown, but I often think longingly of the big backyard in the house where I grew up.

My dad is the gardener in the family. He was a minister in a small town in Saskatchewan before he retired, and he always planted a large vegetable garden to augment what his salary put on the table. Some of his poorer parishioners also shared in the harvest.

But his flowers were grown for love and with wonder for the workings of God.

"They have no use," he told me once, when I was about seven. "How wonderful of Him to create something just for our pleasure."

Then he stuck his finger in the air, almost comically, and raised up on his knees.

"Consider the lilies of the field, how they grow; they toil not, neither do they spin: and yet I say this unto you, that even Solomon in all his glory was not arrayed like one of these."

Then he looked at my surprised face, chuckled, and sank back to his knees in the dirt.

"Matthew," he explained. Matthew who? I wondered.

Gardening was also a form of meditation for him, time taken out of his duties for contemplation. I wonder how many sermons were composed while he was on his knees in the dirt. I know he had a harder time writing them in the winter, when the garden was buried in snow.

From the time I could toddle I was his helper. Family albums are full of pictures of me in the garden: staggering around with a watering-can when I was three; standing proudly on a stepladder next to a sunflower I grew myself from seed; smelling roses in my smocked party dress.

Gardening was the special time that I had my father all to myself, away from my older brother and sister, away from my mother, away from his parishioners. He was a reserved man, but the hours we shared in the garden made me feel loved and special. It was a great gift he gave me. The gift of peace.

The first thing I did when I bought this house with Mickey, my former lover, was to take a sledge-hammer to the old concrete patio and reclaim the space for growing things. After five years, it is starting to come together. Last summer the perennials I planted that first season had filled the small yard with blooms until the fall. Vegetables are out of the question, of course, but I'd had plenty of herbs to dry and use through the winter. I wish my job didn't take me away from home so often in the summer.

I love Toronto. Even though I grew up in a small town on the prairies, I can't do without the energy of a big city. But I also can't do without a garden. And sometimes, late at night, when I hear the whistle from a freight train on the tracks going up the Don Valley, I have a longing for my other home. If I could just hop that freight I could ride it to the grain elevator six blocks from the house I grew up in.

I got the rake out of the garage. It was really rushing the season to do much, but the glorious weather made me want to get my hands in the dirt. Besides, I had a few things to think about and, like my father, I found gardening good for rumination.

I raked the soft, decomposing leaves off the flower beds and put them on the compost heap beside the house. The pale green shoots of tulips were poking through the earth, and there were buds on the forsythia bush.

"We've survived another winter, chum," I said to Elwy, who was rolling in the dirt.

The work lifted my gloom a bit. With the sun on my shoulders and the rich, dark smell of earth in my nostrils, it was hard to feel sorry for myself.

I thought about my dad, imagining him doing the same things in his garden. He wouldn't be, though. He is a lot more sensible than I am. Premature bursts of spring are seductive, but he would be mindful of the real possibilities of a good old prairie blizzard lurking beyond the big horizon.

Then I thought about Andy. He's like my father in some ways, strange as that may seem. I think they would like each other if they met. They are both methodical, careful men, with deep passions. They are both driven by a sense of what is right, and by a strong commitment to justice. Andy, like my father, is a gentle man, even though he works in a world of violence.

And both put their career before anything else. It used to drive my mother wild that Daddy was always on call. It was a rare supper that wasn't interrupted by the telephone, at least.

"They are troubled souls," he would say. "How can I deny them?"

"They'll still be troubled after you finished eating," she would answer.

"I won't be a minute," he would say, always. And usually he would reappear half an hour later, get his plate out of the warming oven, and finish his meal.

My mother always sat with him then, while we kids did the dishes. I think she liked those times, the way I did the times in the garden.

But I'm not my mother, unfortunately, and I can't tailor my life to my man's.

I guess I could be more understanding, though. That's assuming I want this relationship to last. It's such hard work.

And he's a cop. I don't like cops. Look at the guys he hangs around with. They're all right-wingers. Andy voted for Brian Mulroney last time around, for God's sake. I've never dared ask him how he feels about capital punishment. How can I be in love with a guy who is probably in favour of capital punishment?

I can't, obviously, but I am.

I was pruning the rose bushes following this futile train of thought when T.C. came home from school. He brought a couple of his baseball gloves and a ball into the garden.

"Want to play catch? I've got to get my arm in shape."

"Why not?"

"Do you want to go to the park?"

"No, I'm not ready to take this show public quite yet. We can play in the driveway. I get the end with the garage. I'm not going to chase the ones I miss."

T.C. has been trying to teach me how not to throw like a girl since he and Sally moved in. It hasn't worked, but at least I don't make a complete fool of myself when I have to throw a stray ball to a player.

Besides, there's no one else to play with him. Sally is allergic to sports and his father's only around the odd weekend.

"You're getting stronger," I yelled down the driveway. "That last one really stung. Are you on steroids or something?"

He flexed his skinny biceps and grinned.

"I'm almost ready for the big leagues," he shouted.

After half an hour I begged off.

"I'm getting too old for this nonsense," I said.

"Do you want to hit me some ground balls?" he asked.

"Are you kidding? Don't push your luck."

He accepted my refusal gracefully enough. By the time I was back in the kitchen, he was bouncing a tennis ball off the garage door.

CHAPTER

18

At 6:00, I took advantage of the cheap rates and phoned my parents. We spent half an hour catching up on all the family news, with one of them on each extension. My father kept worrying about the money I was spending.

Then I made myself some grilled cheese sandwiches with my mum's bread-and-butter pickles on the side and had supper listening to the sports phone-in show on the Titan radio network.

At game time, Elwy and I climbed the stairs to my study and hit the couch in front of the television. Half my attention was on a book, the other half on the ballgame. Elwy was more interested in washing himself and trying to make me pat him. I obliged, and he curled up on my lap and stayed, a great black-and-white dead weight, until I moved him an hour later when both legs had gone to sleep. The Titans beat the Tigers, 8–3. Joe went three for four.

Things got more lively at midnight, when the phone began to ring. The early edition of the *Planet* had just hit the street. The first call came from Keith Jarvis, my competitor at the *Mirror*.

"What the hell is going on?" he asked. He sounded a bit drunk. "The desk just tracked me down and told me to match your story about Joe Kelsey. He's a fag?"

"Good luck," I said.

Matching is a reporter's nightmare. When a paper has been clearly scooped by the opposition, it has to cover its ass by having some version of the story or risk looking stupid.

"Kelsey's line has been busy for the past half hour," Jarvis complained. "They want me to go to his apartment and talk to him."

"Well, I guess this is my payback for the trade you scooped me on last November."

"Is this for real?"

"It's all there in the story."

"I haven't seen it yet."

"Well, I'm sure you will find it interesting. But I'm going to have to let you go now. Busy day tomorrow."

The next call was from Joe. I told him he would probably get a better night's sleep if he took his phone off the hook and told the concierge that he wasn't to be disturbed, and said I'd see him at the ballpark in the morning.

There were a few more: from Bill Sanderson of the *World*, from the wire services, from *Sports Illustrated*, *Maclean's* magazine. At 1:30 I followed my own advice and turned off the ringers on my phones and let the answering machine take over, with a new message: "This is Kate Henry. I have nothing to add to what I have already written. It's late and I want some sleep. I'll be at the ballpark tomorrow. Please leave a message."

Then I slept, fitfully. I was nervous about the next day. Besides, I hadn't got the call I was hoping for. I had probably blown it totally with Andy.

The next morning it was Ernie Banks weather – a great day, let's play two – a glorious balmy spring morning, which made up a little bit for my weariness.

The *Planet* was waiting on the doorstep. My story shared front-page billing with Margaret Papadakis's: DO YOU KNOW THE DAYLIGHT STALKER? In the story, Staff Sergeant Munro, head of the investigation, asked any citizen who had seen anyone, even a loved one, behaving strangely, to contact the police. He talked about the history and profiles common to many serial killers, about possible behaviour to watch for.

"This man could have a wife," he said. "He may live with a family. Please, if you suspect someone, even someone close to you, call our hot-line. If he isn't stopped, he will kill again. This man needs help."

The story got smaller play than mine, which says something about our priorities.

I drove past Joe's building on the way to the ballpark. There were television crews staking out the front door. I hoped Joe had the sense to leave by another exit.

There were more crews at the ballpark. Timing is everything, of course, and it happened that the

Titans and Tigers were going to play the NBC Game of the Week. Bert Nelson, their colour commentator, looking a little hungover around the eyeballs, pulled me aside as soon as he saw me.

"Kate, great to see you again," he began. We had exchanged not more than ten words in our entire relationship, but suddenly I was his big buddy.

"It was a remarkable feat to get this story. Indubitably the scoop of the season," he said. He'd obviously been watching old Howard Cosell tapes in his spare time. "I'd like you to come on air and tell our viewers how you did it."

"Why don't you talk to Joe? It's his story."

"Well, to be absolutely frank with you, he isn't a particularly articulate player."

"Really? I don't find that."

Nelson, of course, had never spoken with Joe. He only talked to the big-name guys. His assumption, although I might be unfair, was that because Joe was black he couldn't mumble his way out of a gym bag.

"Besides, he's having a heck of a season. That alone would be worth talking to him about. Give it a try, Bert. If he won't talk, come back to me, but I'd rather not."

I'd had my share of being the story rather than the reporter when I first got into this business. First time in every city in the league someone was sent out to the stadium to do the woman-in-the-locker-room story. It really got in the way of my doing my job, which was hard enough without having cameras following me into the clubhouse. Besides, the players began to complain that I was getting all the ink.

But, in the absence of any Titan players on the field, I was in the thick of things again. After ten minutes of being interviewed by other reporters, I decided to escape. I tried to go into the clubhouse, but the attendant at the door told me that there was a team meeting going on. No press allowed. No kidding.

And no comment when the meeting broke up. Most of the players, some looking shocked, others angry, brushed past us and went immediately to work, shagging fly balls and waiting their turns in the batting cage. Red O'Brien came into the dugout long enough to pin up the lineup, then went back inside. I took a peek. Joe was pencilled in at his normal spot. Good.

I went in to the clubhouse complex. A few players were standing around their lockers. I poked my head in the door, looking for Joe. He wasn't there. Stinger Swain spotted me.

"Get that bitch out of here," he shouted.

"It's a joy to see you, too, Stinger," I said.

Kelsey wasn't in the lounge or weight room. That left the trainer's room and O'Brien's office. Both doors were shut, so I leaned against a wall in the corner of the corridor where I could keep an eye on both the doors.

Five minutes later, Joe came out of Red's office and smiled nervously at me.

"So far, not bad," he said. "I'm playing, anyway, and Red says he doesn't care what happens off the field as long as I can produce between the white lines."

"That's all you can ask for. What about the other guys? How did they react?"

"I told Tiny and Eddie and Gloves after the game last night. They were pretty good. They couldn't believe it at first."

"You had a team meeting. Was it about this?"

"Yeah. Some of them were pretty hot. Stinger was the worst."

"Surprise, surprise."

"Yeah," he laughed, shakily. "He said there's no way he's going to play on the same team with a faggot. He wants a trade. You'll be glad to know that he also said he wouldn't go in the shower when I was there."

"I can understand that. Stinger is so attractive that you'd have a hard time keeping your hands off him. Shucks, I know I have that problem all the time."

Joe was relaxing the more I made jokes, but he tensed when four or five other reporters came into the clubhouse.

"Good luck," I muttered.

"I'm going to need it," he replied.

Once the scrum got there, there was an awkward pause while the reporters tried to overcome their embarrassment and phrase the first question.

"Joe, is today's story in the *Planet* true?"

"Is that something like 'Say it ain't so, Joe?' Yes. It is so."

"Why did you wait so long before going public?" said one of the press gang.

"Why did you go public now?" asked another.

"How do you think this will affect your game?"

"What did your team-mates have to say?"

"Do you think the fans will accept you?"

"Whoa," said Joe. "I can't answer all your questions at once. Besides, I've got a game to prepare for. I'll answer your questions later. Now, please excuse me."

He headed down the corridor towards the door to the dugout, all of us in hot pursuit, cameramen jostling for an angle. At the door, he paused, took a deep breath.

"Here goes," he said to me, quietly.

A silence fell on the field when he jogged to the outfield with his glove. It was broken by a derisive wolf whistle from the Tiger dugout. I couldn't see who did it.

I sat in the dugout and watched the usual heavy-handed kidding around while the Titans took batting practice and the Tigers played pepper in front of their dugout. This time, although nobody talked about Joe, there was an edge to the tomfoolery. When he came in for his turn at the cage, everybody stopped talking.

I watched one of Bert Nelson's gophers approach Joe, who shook his head. Soon Bert looked my way, then waved. I shrugged and walked over to where he had his camera set up.

"Do I get the fifty-dollar bill afterwards, just like the players? On my salary, I can use it more than they can."

"We'll see how you do, first," he said.

I ran my fingers through my hair, hoping I was putting it in some sort of order.

"Katherine Henry, you wrote the story that has shocked all of baseball. When did Joe Kelsey make his astonishing revelation to you?"

"Earlier this week. He decided that he no longer wanted to hide the fact of his homosexuality."

"Had you suspected anything about his secret?"

"Since the end of last season, I had been aware of an incident in his past that had led to blackmail."

"You hadn't been tempted to reveal this information sooner?"

"I didn't see why it was anybody else's business, frankly. It had nothing to do with Joe as a player."

"So you protected him?"

"I didn't see it that way."

"Did you try to talk him out of going public when he came to you this week?"

"I asked him if he was ready to handle a lot of criticism, but the decision was his to make, not mine."

"Were you as amazed as the rest of us?"

"Not particularly. I'm sure Joe's not the only gay player in the game, just the only one who has had the courage to talk about it."

"You really think there might be more?"

"Anybody who doesn't has to be awfully naive."

Bert did his best to look worldly.

"What do you think the reaction will be to Joe's confession?"

"I would hope it would be one of indifference, frankly, but I doubt it will be. It will certainly be interesting."

"Katherine Henry, thank you very much."

"You're most welcome."

We shook hands. His had a fifty folded in it.

Once the game started, fan reaction was mixed. Joe got a bigger than usual hand when the lineup was announced, mixed with some catcalls and ribald remarks. I spent the first few innings in the stands eavesdropping. I even talked to strangers. Of the dozen fans I interviewed, only a few were negative. Those thought he should be kicked out of the game.

"It sets a bad example for the kids," said one middle-aged woman with a tight mouth. "They look up to baseball players, and you shouldn't look up to filth like him."

Her husband nodded his head in agreement. He was wearing a peaked cap with a plastic dog turd on the brim, and a tee-shirt that read "Golfers do it in the rough."

"How can he call himself a Christian?" he asked.

On the other hand, an elderly couple, from whom I expected shock, just shrugged.

"Different strokes for different folks," said the husband, as the wife nodded approval. Amazing.

And no one I talked to was unaware of the story. Strangers who recognized me wanted to talk about it. Several of them expressed touching concern for Joe's well-being.

Joe singled his first time at bat. When Sugar Jenkins, coaching at first base, reached over to give him the usual pat on the bum, he stopped in mid-gesture and contented himself with clapping his hands and shouting encouragement.

This did not go unnoticed. One yahoo over the dugout amused his cronies by shouting, "What's the matter, Jenkins, afraid you'll get AIDS?" Big yucks, all around.

Someone else yelled "Come on, Josephine, steal a base!"

That one was so popular it got picked up all around the stadium and was used intermittently throughout the game. There were also remarks about how he threw like a girl whenever he warmed up between innings in left field. But it was all pretty tame stuff. This was, after all, the home crowd. Detroit, next week, would be a different story.

I looked over at Sandy, sitting behind home plate, but didn't go and talk to him. I figured someone might recognize me and make the connection.

Joe responded with aplomb. He ignored the taunts when in the field and at the plate, and went three for four with a home run. The Titans won, and I followed the herd down the elevators to the club-house.

It was quiet in there, more subdued than after

most wins. Most of the reporters went in to see the manager, but I wanted to get to the players first.

Most of them were surprisingly noncommittal. They were obviously shocked and alarmed. It was as if Joe had somehow turned against them. He had joined a group they considered disgusting. I'm sure that more than a couple of them were replaying in their heads all the crude jokes about homosexuals they had made in his hearing. But most of them had been Joe's friend for years. His announcement couldn't change that.

"To tell you the truth, I'd rather I didn't know," said Tiny Washington. "But I don't see what it has to do with what he does on the field."

"I've always assumed that some ballplayers are gay," Gloves Gardiner said. "I'm surprised Joe is one of them, but I admire his guts for admitting it."

Stinger Swain was predictable. "It makes me sick. He doesn't belong in baseball. I've told my agent to get me out of here. I'm not going to play with some pervert."

His crony, relief pitcher Goober Grabowski, provided good-old-boy humour with comments about dropping soap in the shower and other original remarks. I remembered the road trip last year when I had shared the elevator with the two of them and a pair of giggling blonde twins who couldn't have been more than seventeen. But, hey, that's just normal behaviour, right? Male bonding in action.

For his part, Joe said he would rather talk about his game. He explained that due to the large number of requests for interviews from all over, he would hold a press conference on Monday, an off-day.

The reporters seemed almost relieved to go back to their usual questions about what type of pitch he had hit for the home run.

I popped my head into Hugh Marsh's office to see what the outside response had been.

"Calls from all over the place," he said. "We've been swamped all day. People want to interview him, send him messages of encouragement or hate. Sick Kids' Hospital is having an emergency board meeting to see if they should cancel his visit next week. It's nuts. Why didn't he just stay in the closet? It would have made my job a lot easier."

Poor baby.

"Oh, listen, we've made a player move. Owl Wise has to go on the fifteen-day disabled list with his ankle. It's just not healing. We're bringing up Watanabe."

A Japanese player in the big leagues. That ought to take some of the attention off Joe. Hugh handed me a stats sheet. The kid was hitting .332 after a few weeks in Triple A and hadn't made an error. One stolen base in two attempts. He'd been a pretty good base runner at spring training.

"Should be interesting," I said. "I guess I'd better brush up on my Japanese."

On my way back to the press box I ran into Joe coming out of the clubhouse, alone. I walked with him to the exit.

"Are you okay?"

"It wasn't too bad," he said.

"Listen, do you and Sandy want to come over for dinner on Monday after your press conference? Just a small group. Sally and T.C., Andy if he's around. Family."

"That would be great. I'll check with Sandy and tell you tomorrow."

I watched him go through the gate. The kids, pens at the ready for autographs, stepped silently out of his way.

Damn.

CHAPTER

20

When I got home at 6:30 there was a note from Sally on my door, inviting me down to supper. The best offer I'd had all day. I dropped my gear and kicked off my reporter shoes as soon as I got in the door. Elwy came padding out of the bedroom, yawning, and rolled over on his back at my feet.

"Another hard day, eh, Fatso? Busy, busy, busy, moving from one soft spot to another. What a guy."

He meowed indignantly, then got to his feet and walked towards his empty bowl in the kitchen. I followed him.

"Well, sure. After a day like that, you must be starving."

I spooned the food into his bowl, then punched up Sally's number on the kitchen phone while he wolfed it down.

"So, the queen of Queen Street West hasn't got a hot Saturday night date?" I asked, when she answered.

"No, it was just that I had so many offers I couldn't decide which one deserved the honour of my acceptance," she said. "Are you on?"

"I happen to be free of engagements myself," I laughed. "What time do you want me?"

"How about right now."

"Can I bring anything?"

"I've got it under control."

"We'll be down in a minute."

"We?"

"I thought I'd bring Elwy. I haven't been giving him much attention lately."

"I haven't got that much food," Sally laughed.

"It's okay. He is dining as we speak."

"Then he's welcome. See you soon."

I hung up my work clothes and changed into jeans and a sweatshirt. On the way out the door with Elwy, I remembered to check my answering machine. There were two messages. The first was Sally, inviting me to supper. The second was Andy.

"I got your message. Sorry I didn't get back to you sooner. It's five. I guess you're still at work. I'll call again later. I don't know where I'll be. Bye."

I tried to reach him, but he wasn't at his office or home. At least he'd called. I changed my message, leaving Sally's number, and went downstairs. Sally was in the kitchen slicing tomatoes. I deposited Elwy on a chair and hugged her.

"Pour yourself a glass of wine," she said. "There's white plonk in the fridge and red plonk on the table. Is Sanelli's pizza and a salad all right with you?"

"For something completely different," I said, pouring myself some red, slightly less plonkish than the white. Sally has no discernible taste buds when it comes to wine. "Where's T.C.?"

"He should be back any minute. He's out with that friend of yours from work."

"Who?"

"That guy that writes about kids' sports. He's doing a piece on T.C.'s baseball team. Is he ever thrilled!"

"Oh, God, not Dickie Greaves."

"He seemed nice. He came by and picked T.C. up to take him to the park for a picture. He's cute, too."

"You wouldn't think so if you worked at the next desk," I said. "Besides, he's too young for my tastes."

"I've got nothing against cradle robbing," Sally said.

"And he's married."

"Oh," Sally said. "Happily, I suppose."

"With a new bouncing baby boy and all," I said.

"Oh, well, at least he's made my kid's day. How was yours? Big story today."

"Don't tell me you actually read something I wrote."

Sally is not a sports fan.

"It was a great story. I can't believe the guy came out of the closet."

I had just begun to tell her about the reaction at the ballpark when T.C. arrived home, looking very pleased with himself. Dickie was with him.

"Hi, Kate. It's an unexpected treat to see you," he said. "This young friend of yours is quite a kid."

"Would you like a glass of wine?" Sally asked, smiling at his charm, the silly woman.

"Well, just one. I have to get home to my own boy," he said, then sat beside me at the table.

"That was quite a story, Kate. Congratulations."

"Thanks."

"It took guts."

"How so?"

"Not you, Kate. Kelsey."

"He's got a lot of courage," I agreed.

"Kate was just telling me that things got pretty rough at the ballpark," Sally said. "Red or white?"

"White if you have it."

"It wasn't that bad," I said. "I thought the fans were pretty fair."

"What happened?" T.C. asked. He looked a bit uncomfortable.

"Just some guys yelling things. Heckling him."

"It will probably be worse on the road," Dickie said.

"Well, I just think it's gross," T.C. blurted.

"Why?" I asked, exchanging a glance with Sally. Time for a little lesson in tolerance.

"All the kids say gay people are sick," he said.

"Well, all the kids are wrong, then," Sally said.

"Oh, yeah? What about that guy who's killing kids?"

"That's stupid, T.C., that's not all gay people," Sally said. "That man is a monster. Maybe he's gay, maybe he's not. But there are gay ministers and teachers and doctors, all kinds of gay people. Just like there are bad and good people who aren't gay. What about Marc, at the gallery? He's gay and you like him. He's not sick. Come on, T.C., you know better than that."

"I guess so."

"It's just prejudice, T.C.," I said. "Like people who think that all black people are stupid or all women can't drive or all Chinese people are smart. You can't judge a whole group of people as if they are all the same."

"Yeah," he said, not sounding convinced.

"Come on. You and Joe are buddies. You liked him yesterday, didn't you? You thought he was a good player and a nice guy, right?"

"Yeah."

"He was gay yesterday, too, except you didn't know it. So what's the difference?"

"Nothing, I guess."

"Right. Now go wash up for supper."

"It's tough on kids like T.C.," I said, after he had left the room.

"I can think of a lot of grownups who aren't going to have an easy time adjusting to it, either," Dickie said. "Some of whom we work with."

"I can't imagine Harry taking it too kindly," I laughed.

"And what about the other players?" Sally asked. "Are they going to be waiting for him with baseball bats in a dark alley somewhere?"

"Some of them are freaking out," I said. "Others are being surprisingly enlightened. But I suspect it's going to be a big story for the next few weeks."

"I envy you," Dickie said. "I wish I could get a scoop like that."

"A scandal in the sandlots?" I asked, not too kindly.

"Something like that," he said, then finished his glass of wine. "And there will be a scandal in my house if I don't get home. Thanks for the loan of your son, Sally. It was a pleasure meeting you."

He got up as T.C. came back into the kitchen. They shook hands.

"Kate will let you know when the article is going to run," he said. "Her story is going to be filling the paper for the next few days."

"Do I detect a trace of beat envy?" I asked, keeping it light. "A little bitterness from the kiddie corner?"

"Bitter? Me? Don't be silly," he said. "I love my work. Just because I make less money than you, never get to travel, and get buried in the back of the section, I'm not complaining."

"Go home, Dickie. Take the rest of the weekend off," I said. "You work too hard."

"Easy for you to say," he said. "Some of us have to work for our stories. See you Monday."

T.C. saw him to the door.

"He really does go at it too hard," I said to Sally. "There's no reason for him to be working today. I think it makes him feel important."

"You were pretty hard on the poor guy," Sally said.

"Save your sympathy, Sally," I said. "The poor, put-upon junior reporter is carving out quite a little empire for himself. He's a nice enough guy, but he gets on my nerves in anything but small doses."

T.C. came back into the room.

"That was really fun, Mum," he said. "Mr. Greaves is nice. He bought me a Coke and asked me questions about everything."

"And probably spoiled your appetite for supper," Sally grumped.

"Not a chance," he said. "I'm starved. When do we eat?"

"Soon. Pizza is ready to go in the oven. You're making the salad. I'm sitting down and talking to Kate."

"I hope you don't plan to keep on treating me like your personal slave when I have my picture in the paper," he said.

"Why, of course not," his mother answered. "Then I'll treat you like a very famous slave."

"I never get any respect," he groaned.

"I respect you,'" I said. "I respect you so much that I will allow you to make salad for me. I won't let just anybody do that."

"Thanks a lot," he said, then added, casually, "Where's Andy tonight?"

"Good question!" Sally said, like a *Family Feud* contestant.

So I told them the story and they told me what a bum he was. What are friends for, anyway?

I was surprised by the knock on the door. Andy?

"Will you get that, T.C.?" Sally asked, casually.

"Do I have to?" he asked, then slouched down the hall telegraphing disapproval with every step.

I gave Sally a questioning look.

"David said he might drop by," she explained.

"That explains the glad rags," I said.

David Pelham was short and wiry, good-looking in a socialist sort of way: all beard and corduroy. I'd seen him or his twin a million times at NDP church basement socials. He came into the kitchen carrying a bottle of the currently fashionable Canadian wine and a bouquet of flowers that he had obviously picked up at the fruit store up the street. Carnations. But, hey, flowers are flowers. Sally blushed sweetly to receive them. T.C. looked at me and rolled his eyes, then left the room, muttering something insincere about homework.

We were introduced, and he gave me a firm handshake.

"Did Sally tell you what a great admirer I am?" he asked. "I'm a big ball fan. That was some story about Kelsey. A bit sensationalist, but good. So what's it going to do to morale? I don't like the way things have been going so far."

"It's too early to panic," I said. "There's no one running away with the division."

"I knew I shouldn't get you two together," Sally said, pouring him some wine. "And with T.C., I'm really outnumbered."

"No shop talk," I said. "I'm off duty."

"Thank you, Lord," Sally muttered.

Dinner was strained. T.C. obviously wasn't pleased with a new man in his mother's life, and didn't bother to conceal it.

David tried to include him in the conversation, but T.C. answered in grunts and excused himself from the table the minute he had swallowed the last piece of pizza. Some of the tension left the room with him.

"Sorry about that," Sally said. "I think he's going through a jealous phase."

"It's understandable," David said.

"Thanks for being so understanding."

"Of course, adolescents are your business, aren't they?" I asked.

"Yes, T.C. is a pleasure compared to some of the kids I deal with," he said. "I'm used to rejection."

"Where do you work? Mainly inner-city schools?" I asked.

"There's a middle-class assumption for you. I have a contract with the school board. They send me to wherever they have problems. It's not just poor kids who are fucked up."

"Do you deal with those middle-class gang kids?"

"Among others," he said.

"What effect are these murders having in the schools?" Sally asked. "Are kids scared?"

"They're scared and confused," David said. "There's a certain amount of bravado among the older kids who are trying to be tough. But the kids who knew the victims are having serious problems."

"It's awful " Sally said. "Did you know that Kate is close with the detective in charge of the investigation?"

"Really," he said. "I bet you've got all the inside dirt. What aren't they telling us?"

I shot Sally a glance.

"I don't know anything except what I read in the papers," I said.

"Yeah, I bet," David said.

I looked at my watch. It was only 9:30. My, how time doesn't fly when you're not having much fun. I hung in for another hour of fairly earnest conversation, trying to figure out what this bore's attraction was. Maybe he was great in bed. At 10:30 I decided it was safe to depart without insulting Sally.

"I'm really sorry, but I've got to go," I said, insincerely. "Day game tomorrow."

They didn't try to stop me. But when I got upstairs, the only message on my machine spooked me so much that I went back down and got them. We listened to it together.

The man's voice was gravelly, flat, and uninflected, like someone trying to imitate a robot. Under the circumstances, it was not a voice I recognized.

"Well, Ms. Henry," he said, "it seems you have to help the police again. The first step would be to look under your front door mat."

The beep made us jump.

146

"Let's go look," Sally said.

We went to the front door together, Elwy at our heels. The street was empty. I lifted the mat gingerly. There was an envelope with my byline, carefully clipped out of the paper, pasted to it. Elwy sniffed at it, then wandered off to sit at the top of the steps. I dropped the mat back into place without touching the note.

"Maybe I'd better make a phone call," I said.

"This looks like a job for Staff Sergeant Munro," Sally agreed, dropping her voice at least an octave. As we went up the stairs, she was humming the theme from *Dragnet*.

Andy was at the office. I told him about the note.

"Don't touch it," he said. "I'll have someone there in five minutes. Stay inside, but watch the street. When the uniforms arrive, don't let them touch anything. They're more likely to screw it up than help."

He hung up without saying goodbye. Sally and David sat on the couch while I hovered by my living-room window, feeling like an old biddy, peeking through the blinds. A patrol car was there within minutes. Two constables, a man and a woman, walked up the path together, hands on holsters. They didn't ring the bell. I went down and opened the door anyway.

"Do you want to come in?"

"We'll just wait here, Miss. We have to secure the scene. Please don't come out onto the porch."

I closed the door. Sally and David joined me in the hall.

"I sure hope this isn't just some kind of joke. I'd

hate to see them use up all their cop equipment for nothing."

"Not to mention getting Andy pissed off," said Sally.

I didn't think there was much chance of that. The last time I had opened an envelope full of evidence without calling him first, around the time of the Titan murders, he had given me royal shit.

We were still watching out the window in the front door. When Andy arrived, Sally and David went back to her apartment.

"I'll be up for a while if you need me to give evidence," she whispered. "And I want you to remember this next time you accuse me of meddling in your love life."

I opened the door again. Andy and Jim were on the front walk. Andy was holding Elwy, who looked pleased with himself.

"Hello, gentlemen," I said.

"Hi, Kate. Nice to see you again," said Jim, cheerfully. Andy nodded at me as if we had just met. Even Jim looked at him funny.

"Is anyone going to cross the great divide? The note is under the mat."

"We want to make sure there are no footprints on the porch," Jim said.

"I can't see any. I think Sally swept it this morning, though."

We all stood like a bunch of idiots for a minute or so.

"She's right, Andy. It looks clean."

"We'll wait for the identification team," he said.

Another car pulled up as he spoke. Soon there

was a total of seven cops on my front lawn, staring at the porch. Under Andy's direction, they photographed the scene, lifted the mat, photographed the letter on the porch, spread around a whole bunch of powder, and generally messed things up, looking very efficient and pleased with themselves the whole while.

"I assume the official police cleaning-lady is on her way," I said. Andy didn't look amused.

"You might as well come in," I said. "I'll put on a pot of coffee."

"We can't stay, Kate," Andy said.

"Of course we can," said Jim, stepping inside. "The note is addressed to Kate, after all. I think we can show it to her. Besides, I could use a good cup of coffee. I assume she makes good coffee, right? Otherwise you wouldn't have stuck around her as long as you have."

Either Jim didn't know anything about our fight or he was trying, in a heavy-handed way, to help. Whatever his motivation, I could have kissed him for babbling on the way he was doing. I ran up the stairs and filled the kettle.

"Come sit in the kitchen," I said.

"Nice place you've got, Kate," said Jim, settling his bulk into one of the kitchen chairs.

Measuring coffee into the grinder, I glanced at Andy. He looked disgruntled. Jim had chosen the chair he usually sat in, but under the circumstances, he wasn't going to object. He brought another chair in from the dining room, leaving "my" chair for me.

"Everyone comfy?" I asked. "It will just take a minute for the coffee to drip through. Let me look at the letter."

Andy pulled a pair of surgical gloves out of his pocket.

"Put these on first," he said.

"What is this? Safe sex?"

"Just put them on. We don't want your fingerprints all over the letter."

"Do you really think that a guy smart enough to pull off these murders and get away with it is stupid enough to leave fingerprints?"

"Just put the damn things on," he said.

"Hey, cool out, Andy," his partner said. "You're among friends."

"I'm sorry," I said. "I shouldn't have kidded around like that. I'll open it now. Or you open it. Whatever."

Andy handed it to me, then smiled sheepishly.

"I'm sorry, too. It isn't you I'm angry with."

Now we were getting somewhere.

"Will you two cut the 'After you, Alphonse' shit and open the damn thing?" Jim said.

I got a knife from the rack and slit the envelope carefully, along the short end. I didn't want to tamper with any possible tongue prints on the flap. It was a one-page letter, cut and pasted like the last one I saw.

"Next time you see your boyfriend, tell him he's not even close. I can't wait for him much longer. Give him a hand. He'll never make it alone. I'm still stalking."

At the top of the page was a picture published in the *Planet* the previous fall, when I was given a civilian citation for my assistance in the Titan murders. While some sort of police public-relations suit looked on, Andy and I shook hands. Typical

Planet hype, and a very embarrassing moment for both of us. We had been together the night before, both overslept, and almost missed the ceremony. Then we had to pretend that we hadn't arrived together.

"Goddamn him," Andy said.

"Getting a little personal, isn't he?" Jim said.

"How does he know to leave it here?" I asked, pouring coffee. "Do you think he's been following you?"

"He must have been."

"Not necessarily," Jim said. "A lot of people know about you two."

"But they don't know where I live."

"You're not in the phonebook?"

"Not by my full name. I changed the listing after the house got broken into once when I was in Florida at spring training. An out-of-town byline is an open invitation to break and enter."

"Well, there are ways he could find out, but I think we have to start operating as if he is watching us."

The phone rang. I got up to answer it.

"Tell Munro to have a nice night," whispered the same voice that had been on the machine. Then he hung up.

I stood for a moment listening to the silence until the dial tone kicked in. Then I hung up, gently, and went back to the table. Jim and Andy were talking, but shut up when I sat down. I guess I looked pretty weird.

"What's the matter?" Andy asked.

It took me a moment to make my voice work.

"It was him. He. Whatever. He said to tell you to have a nice night. Then he hung up."

"Shit," Jim said. Then he stood up.

"It's late. You stay here with Kate, Andy. I'll take the letter down to the office and start the paperwork to get a tap put on her phone. With your permission, of course."

I nodded.

"Do you have another tape for your machine? I'll take the one with his voice on it."

"All right."

"Well, good night, then."

Andy walked to the door with him, then came back and cleared away the coffee things. We were awkward together, our fight still unresolved.

"Jim's a nice guy," I said.

"He's the best partner I've had. I just hope it can last."

"What do you mean?"

"We've been together three years now, and we're a great team. We hardly have to talk. But he's overdue for promotion to staff sergeant. Then I'll have to start from scratch with someone new. That's the way the system works."

He poured two scotches, and handed me one.

"But I'm not going to worry about that tonight."

He took my hand and led me into the living room. We sat on the couch. He took the glass out of my hand and put it on the coffee table, then put his arms around me and held me tight.

"Let's talk about it," he said, after a moment.

I started to cry. What a wimp.

152

CHAPTER

22

We got mutual apologies out of the way quickly enough. I was sorry I'd behaved like an idiot, he was sorry he was so obsessed, and we spent an hour on the couch making amends. Elwy tried to join the fun, but was banished with a gentle kick. He retreated to a nearby chair to watch, disconcerting Andy for only a moment.

"That damn cat's a voyeur," he panted.

"Be fair," I said. "It's the closest he's ever going to come to a sex life."

Later, we took our clothes and drinks into the bedroom. I lit some candles, a belated touch of romance. It was also more flattering than electricity, a factor when you are likely to be compared to Margaret Papadakis.

"Did you have a nice lunch yesterday?" I asked.

"What a waste of time," he said. "I asked her to come down to the station to talk, and she insisted we meet at Orso."

"Who paid?"

"Are you kidding? The police department won't cover a meal like that. Then she came on to me for an hour while I tried to get her to take notes about our appeal to the public."

"Poor baby. It's just that you're so irresistible."

"Kate, it wasn't fun. Trust me."

"Oh, sure. And you had to force down that fabulous food and wine, too, I bet."

"Coffee."

"While Margaret flattered you and told you what a wonderful cop you are."

"She talked about you, too," he said. "I don't think she likes you very much. She kept talking about what good friends you were, but I think she told me every rumour that had ever gone through the newsroom about you."

"Because she is concerned about her good friend." I laughed, insincerely.

"Yes, I found it very interesting. I hadn't realized that you and Sally are lovers. And I can't imagine why you never told me about the time you got drunk on the road and took on the entire Titan outfield and then sent for the relief pitchers."

"That bitch! She didn't!"

"Calm down," he said, pulling me back into his arms. "I didn't tell her any of our secrets. Like how gullible you are."

"You . . ."

He shut me up with a kiss. We both laughed. I lit a cigarette and we sipped our drinks. The silence was warm.

"I missed you," he said.

"It's only been two days."

"It seems longer."

"Yeah."

"You've been busy," he said. "I read your story this morning. It was good. What was the reaction?"

I told him all about it, then asked about his case.

"I spent today with a guy from the FBI who came up from Washington to give us some advice."

"Good advice?"

"Who knows. It was hard to get beyond his ego. He treated me as if I was some hick sheriff with an IQ of seventeen."

"Uh oh. And you?"

"I had to listen. He knows his stuff."

"What does he think?"

"The same thing we do. The killer is apparently normal, is in some kind of position of authority that these kids would trust. He's ready to kill again. He's starting to want to get caught. Big revelations from the hotshot from south of the border."

He sat up in bed.

"Give me a cigarette, will you?"

"You don't smoke."

"I did, for ten years. I just quit a year ago. I want one now."

"If you're sure. I'm certainly in no position to stop you," I said, passing him the pack and the lighter.

He lit one, and took our glasses out to the kitchen. Elwy hopped on the bed. I heard Andy with the ice and bottle. It was going to be a long night.

"This is the crucial period," he said, when he came back. "He's at his most vulnerable now. If we don't catch him, it will be as if we have given him permission to kill again. It's as if the sane part is making one last cry for help. We have to get him soon."

"Maybe you'll be able to trace one of the phone calls. Or maybe there will be fingerprints on the note."

"I can't count on that. Neither can you, for that matter, now that he's sending you notes. What do you want to do? I could get you a bodyguard."

"Oh, no, not that again."

During the Titan murders, a large, eager young constable followed me around for a few days, causing me no end of embarrassment in the press box and locker room.

"I know it cramps your style," he said, "but you're in this now. I don't want you in danger because of me. Not that I think you are. With the profile we're developing on this guy, I don't think you're a target."

"And if I had a bodyguard, it might scare him off trying to get through me to you. Wouldn't it make more sense just to have someone watching the house in case he comes back?"

"That's already taken care of."

I looked at the window, which had no curtains.

"I hope he's not using binoculars," I giggled.

"It would do my reputation some good."

"More than you know," I said, sensing a chance to get back at him for his lunch with Margaret. "You realize that your great and good comrade in arms, Bob Flanagan, refers to you as the faggot?"

"He doesn't."

"Does."

"Why didn't you tell me that before?"

"Oh, now you're offended. When I told you all the filthy things he said to me, that didn't bother you."

"That asshole," he said, really steamed.

"Hey, lighten up, Andy. He's a good cop, just a little rough around the edges."

He pinched me. I pinched back, and we rolled around for a while. Elwy dug in his claws and rode the foot of the bed like a sailor on a stormy sea, determined to hang in this time.

"We've got to go to sleep," I said. "It's three o'clock in the morning. I have to be at the ballpark in seven hours," I said, later.

"Yeah, you're right." Neither of us moved.

"I just can't turn off my brain," he said, after a few moments. "Not while he's out there."

"Mocking you."

"He may be right. I'm getting nowhere. Maybe I ought to get off the case."

"Whoa. Wait a minute. Don't beat yourself up. That's not going to accomplish anything."

"Yes, Mother," he said, then rolled over on his side, away from me.

"You're right," he said, after a moment of silence. "Thanks. I'm just tired and down about the whole thing. Actually, these communications are probably good. I think he's losing it."

"Tell me about it."

He rolled back and propped himself up on the pillows.

"All right, ask questions."

"Have you talked to the parents again?"

"Yeah, but they weren't any help. They are destroying themselves with guilt, but not for any reason. They were good parents. They didn't let their kids run free. They were strict. The Goldmans spoiled them with things, but they had rules. All the kids had to call home if they were changing their plans. It's not as if these were little rebels. They were safe, boring little kids who would never go off with a stranger."

"But you can't find anyone who knew them all."

"There's no connection, I'm as sure of that as I can be. We've been over and over it again."

"Different schools."

"Right."

"What about outside teachers? Music teachers, scout leaders, coaches?"

"Nope."

"Did they play in the same league? Maybe referees."

"We've checked that, too."

"I hate to say it, but what about a cop? Even the most well-trained kids would go with a cop."

"Or someone disguised as a cop. We haven't rejected the possibility. I hope to Christ it's not a cop."

"Priests are suspect these days, but these kids were all different religions. What else?"

"Someone they all look up to. A well-known athlete. A television performer."

"I can't stand to think about it."

"And I can't stop thinking about it."

"Neither can I. But let's try."

I got up, set the alarm for 8:30, and blew out the candles, then got back in under the duvet. We spooned, with his body against my back.

"Good night," he murmured into my neck. "I'm glad I'm here."

"Me, too."

23

"*Konnichi wa?*"

"Emphasis on the first syllable," Andy said. "KON-*nichi wa*. That's hello. During the day. *Konban wa* is for the evening."

"Got it," I said. "*Sayonara* is goodbye. What's please?"

"That depends. *Dōzo* is please, like please go first through the door, or please have this food. If you want a different kind of please –"

"Fine, one's enough for me. I know thank you from Kuri. *Arigatō*, right?"

"Well, yes. Except, if you want to be more polite, it is *dōmo arigatō*. Or more polite still, it's *domō arigatō gozaimasu.*"

"Well, *arigatō* to you for that."

"And casually, it is simply *domō.*"

"Let's get real. How do you casually say 'you're welcome'?"

"Try *dō itashimashite*."

"Then how do you say 'Welcome to Toronto'?"

"*Toronto e yōkoso*. Emphasis on the *yō*."

Sunday, no day of rest for sportswriters or cops on an ugly case, began with a language lesson. I figured that a few words of Japanese might be a good way to start off with the new Titan shortstop.

We covered the basic greetings and terms of politeness over breakfast and were out of the house before 10:00. Even though I arrived early, it was already circus time at the ballpark. I recognized the senior writer for *Sports Illustrated* in the mob around Red O'Brien, and the national baseball writers for the Washington *Post*, Boston *Globe*, and Philadelphia *Inquirer*. It was like the first game of the World Series.

Christopher Morris, my favourite magazine writer, stood by the Tiger dugout surveying the scene. That is his habitual stance, just apart from the crowd, looking at the story from his own angle. That's why he is so good. I went to shake his hand. He kissed me on the cheek.

"Good story, Kate. How did you get it?"

"You've heard of a silver platter?"

"Yes, but he handed it to you, not someone else."

"Just lucky."

"I've been waiting for this for the last few years."

"Joe?"

"No, not him in particular. But there are others."

He mentioned a few: a couple of well-known sluggers and a Cy Young award-winning pitcher. I'd heard rumours about them over the years. He also mentioned the name of one infielder still playing who is known around the league as a real stud, an image he cultivates in a national advertising campaign.

"I can understand why he isn't leaping out of the closet," I laughed. "But the others? What can it hurt now?"

"I don't know. I thought maybe once they were out of the game they might go public."

"Probably worried about the Hall of Fame."

"Yeah, I guess Cooperstown isn't quite ready."

"Not ready? Last time I checked, those guys didn't even know it was the twentieth century."

"Now, Kate, let's not malign our national shrine."

"Your nation, not mine."

"How is Kelsey doing, anyway?"

"Fine. I guess you know he's not talking until tomorrow. Are you going to stick around?"

"Yes. Dinner tonight?"

"Sure. That would be nice. I might bring a friend, too. Listen, since you can't talk to Joe, come with me. I'm on another story right now. Come meet our new Japanese player."

"Who is he?"

"Atsuo Watanabe. He's a shortstop. Ted Ferguson and Red O'Brien signed him last year when they went on the All-Star tour. He's been in Triple A."

"Beats standing around here interviewing other reporters," Christopher said. "Lead on."

Watanabe was leaning over the water fountain in the dugout. The name on his uniform curved around his slim back in an inverted U. His was a name that only a broad-shouldered player could carry well. This kid would have been better off named Smith. As we approached him, he turned around, looking with rookie eyes at everything going on. No matter where he's played before, and Watanabe had played in some pretty grand ballparks in Japan, his first view of a major-league stadium is a thrill. I had seen many rookies at just this moment. Some of them had kept the wonder, others had quickly taken it for granted.

"*Konnichi wa, Watanabe-san*," I said, holding out my hand. "*Toronto e yōkoso*."

He shook it, bowing slightly, amusement in his eyes.

"*Konnichi wa*," he said, then went on, in Japanese, of course. I didn't understand a word. I guess my face showed it.

"I was merely thanking you for the respect you have showed me, Miss Henry," he said, in precise, slightly accented English. "It is very kind of you."

"You speak English very well," I said, a little embarrassed.

"I finished first in my class every year. I was an excellent student of English."

"If I appear surprised, it is only because many of the baseball players in North America do not appear to have been very good students."

The formality of his speech was catching.

"I have learned this in my short time here. I have been anxious to talk about literature and political theory with my team-mates, but they have not shared the interest."

"You are familiar with North American literature?" Christopher asked, as surprised as I.

"I like the Canadian writers in particular," he

said. "Margaret Atwood, Alice Munro. You have many excellent women writers. I started, of course, with the works of Miss Lucy Maud Montgomery."

Christopher looked at me, confused. He had obviously not grown up on *Anne of Green Gables*. I remembered some things I had read about the Japanese and their fascination with things Canadian.

"All Japanese school children are very familiar with Miss Montgomery's work," Watanabe continued. "Do you think it will be possible for me to go to see her famous home on the off-day tomorrow?"

His face fell when I explained that Prince Edward Island is 2,000 kilometres away from Toronto.

"And I'm afraid that the Rocky Mountains are out of the question, too," I said. "But you could handle a day-trip to Niagara Falls. Perhaps Hugh Marsh could arrange it."

"Thank you so much," he said.

"*Dō itashimashite*," I said.

We both laughed.

"Let me ask you some questions about playing in the major leagues," I said. "Is baseball here very different from Japan? I realize it is the same game, but there must be differences."

"Oh, yes. They do not expect players to work so hard here. And the fans are very different. In the minor leagues, very quiet. I will be interested to see how major-league fans behave this afternoon. This stadium, will it be full?"

"On a Sunday afternoon, probably. There will be a lot of fans here from Detroit, too."

"They will be the ones making all the noise," Christopher said. "The Titan fans aren't typical major-league fans. They are Canadians, more polite than most. Wait until you come to New York next week."

"Ah, Yankee Stadium. It is my dream to play there since I was a little boy."

"That's not typical either," I said, "Whatever Christopher tells you. They don't call it the Bronx Zoo for nothing. There are fewer animals in the rest of the parks."

"Things aren't so quiet in Japan, either. Japanese fans care very passionately for their teams. For even a high-school championship, the stadiums will be full."

"I'm interested in why you came," said Christopher.

"I would like to bring honour to my country by playing well in the major leagues."

"Your family must be very proud," I said.

Watanabe frowned.

"No, they are ashamed of me," he said. "They think I am betraying them and my country to play with the *gaijin* – the foreigners. I must do very well here to win back their respect."

Then he smiled.

"But I think I will do very well."

"This is not a typical Japanese attitude, I don't think," Christopher said.

"And that is why I am playing baseball here and not in Japan," Watanabe replied.

"Well, good luck to you," I said. "I'll see you after the game. You realize that women reporters come into the dressing room, don't you?"

"I have been told," he smiled. "I have brought a

yukata – robe – with me. You will excuse me now, please. It is time for my batting practice."

We exchanged handshakes and bows. Watanabe ran to the cage, where other starting players were waiting their turn. Most of them ignored him. He struck up a conversation with Joe Kelsey.

"I wonder if he knows he is talking to a pariah," Christopher said.

"Misfittery loves company," I said.

CHAPTER

24

Atsuo Watanabe's major-league debut wasn't exactly out of the story books. His first major-league hit, and his only hit in the game, bounced on a seam in the turf over the third baseman's head for a cheap double.

"He should be ashamed to put that ball in his trophy case," said Jeff Glebe, who had given up his day off to try to find a new angle on the Kelsey story for his column.

"It will be a hit in the box score tomorrow," I said. "What are you, a purist?"

As we chatted, Watanabe got picked off second.

"Welcome to the big leagues," said Jeff.

He made up for his rookie blunder on the basepaths with his defensive play. He made one terrific diving catch in the hole to rob a Tiger of a base hit. He was warmly received by the fans.

The Titans won 4-1, their fifth in a row.

"Things are looking up," I said, as Jeff and I headed towards the elevator after the game.

"Don't hurt yourself jumping on the band-wagon."

It was jammed, as usual, in the elevator. We crowded on, with apologetic smiles for Cecil. Because the elevator serves not only the press box, but the high-rollers in the private boxes one floor down and the wheelchair patrons on the main stadium level, service is intermittent at best, just after a game, and it's a long walk down the stairs.

"Up, please," said Bill Sanderson, at the back of the elevator. He didn't get a laugh. He never did.

We landed with a thump at the ground floor. The doors didn't open. We waited for several endless seconds in silence. Cecil pushed several buttons with some urgency.

"Too much weight," he said, looking pointedly at me and Jeff, the last two on.

"Oh, Christ," Jeff said. "My claustrophobia has just kicked in."

He wasn't kidding. For the next twenty minutes he was chalk white and sweating. I don't know what he was worried about. At least he was tall enough to breathe up there. I leaned against the door and pretended I was somewhere else and that I didn't have to pee. As the minutes passed, the place began to stink from everybody's nervous sweat.

By the time we were rescued, most of us were ready to throttle Sanderson, who had babbled non-stop about deadlines and the depletion of the oxygen supply. The only one I was worried about was Cecil. I thought he was a bit old for the stress, but he was completely cool. In fact, whenever I began to lose it, all I had to do was look at him. He would give me a little smile or a wink. In fact, after they pried the doors open, he wanted to go right back up to pick up the wheelchair patrons.

By the time we got to the clubhouse, most of the players had dressed. There was tension in the air.

"What went on here?" I asked one of the wire-service reporters who had obviously taken the stairs.

"It happened before I got here, too," he said. "I had to file before I came down. There was some sort of fight, I think."

I looked for Gloves Gardiner, the catcher, my most reliable informant. I saw him coming out of the trainer's room and intercepted him in the corridor.

"Stinger started it," he said, wearily. "I wouldn't tell you except that Keith Jarvis was there, and if it's in the *Mirror*, you might as well have it, too."

The *Mirror* is a muckraking tabloid with the journalistic standards of a Brussels sprout.

Evidently Stinger had seen Atsuo Watanabe talking to Joe Kelsey and had made one of his usual crude remarks. This had confused Watanabe and enraged Joe, who slugged Swain. Before the fight broke up, ten guys had been involved.

"You, too, Gloves?"

He fingered the bruise on his cheek and nodded.

"Who else?" I asked.

"Tiny tried to break it up, but Goober Grabowski ganged up with Stinger. When he hit Tiny, Eddie Carter and I got involved. David Sloane came in with Goober and Stinger, then Alex Jones came in with us. I don't know who all was in there at the end."

"Blacks on one side, whites on the other?"

"Except me, and the new kid. But to Stinger and Goober, he probably counts as black."

"What broke it up?"

"Red. He fined our asses, too."

"The *Mirror* is going to go nuts with this," I said.

"I know. See if you can put it in some kind of perspective."

"What would you suggest? When a star third-baseman starts a brawl among members of the same team, I can hardly describe it as a tea party. What is it going to do to morale?"

"Not help it, that's for sure."

"Maybe the off-day will cool some tempers," I said. What are your plans for your twenty-four hours of freedom?"

"Look for a place to live. Karin and the kids will be coming up next month."

"Good luck."

"We could get the same condo we had last year, but she wants something with a yard this time."

"For the kids? I don't blame her," I said.

"I'm going out to Mississauga tomorrow."

Typical. The players, bred in the suburbs of America, have no idea that they can live downtown in Toronto and still have a yard and parks and play-grounds all around them. So they head for the 'burbs even here.

Ah, well, if they didn't, we wouldn't get to have Mississauga Day at the ballpark every year and watch the mayor bounce the ceremonial first pitch after the presentation ceremonies. A fine Titan tradition, and she gives out dandy tee-shirts.

The trainer's room door opened again and Joe Kelsey came out, heading for the exit. I excused myself and ran after him. We stopped in the corridor under the stadium, halfway to the gate, out of sight or earshot of other reporters.

"I don't want to talk about it," he said, wearily.

"You don't have to. I heard the story from Gloves. Can you just give me one quote for my story?"

"Just say that it was a misunderstanding that got out of hand, and that I regret any part I played in it."

"Are you okay?"

"Depressed, more than anything."

"You knew it wasn't going to be easy."

"I just don't like seeing my friends getting involved."

"It beats them not getting involved," I said.

"Yeah, and I appreciate it, too. This is going to make the press conference tomorrow more difficult, isn't it?"

"Probably. It will certainly give it a focus. It will be in all the papers. But maybe it's for the best. At least the enemy has a face now. By the way, are you and Sandy coming to supper tomorrow night?"

"Yes, if you still want us."

"Don't be an asshole. Of course we do. Come by at six. If it's nice, we'll barbecue."

"And no more talking about it?"

"Not if you don't want to. T.C. will want to talk baseball, for sure. If you can stand that."

"It beats sex any day."

"Doing it, or talking about it?"

"Watch your mouth, Kate."

After Joe left, I went back into the clubhouse to find Watanabe. He was alone in front of his locker. His comments were stunning.

"I beg forgiveness from the fans of Toronto for the mistake I made getting picked off second," he said. "I will try very hard never to do that again, and to be worthy of their approval."

Was this guy for real? It was culture clash again. His comments were ludicrous, but why did I wish more of the guys talked like this?

"Don't feel too badly. You won the game."

"I must apologize to Mr. O'Brien, too. I hope he will let me play tomorrow."

"I wouldn't worry about it."

Before I left him, I gave him a card from Kuri's restaurant.

"Introduce yourself to Kuri-san," I said. "Tell him I sent you. He will take care of you."

I went to find Red O'Brien. He was still in his office, with a dozen reporters. I went into the room, leaned against the wall by the door and began taking notes.

". . . That's what I've been saying all along. What someone does away from the ballpark doesn't bother me. Kelsey could be queer for sheep, for all I care. Don't print that. What I'm saying is, as long as a player's behaviour in his private life doesn't affect what goes on here, it's none of my business.

"Today, it did affect what goes on here. I can't have my players fighting with another. They have to play as a team. I've fined every player who was involved, and called a team meeting for Tuesday before the game. I'm giving them the off-day to see if they can figure out how they are going to work this out. If they can't, we'll have to see what moves we can make."

"Are you talking about trading Joe Kelsey?"

"We're not talking about trading anyone. Kelsey did what he did. I don't have to like it, but the organization believes that it's his business, like I said. If that causes problems with other players that can't be worked out, the organization will do what it can to accommodate the requests of any player who wants to leave."

"Have any players demanded to be traded since Kelsey came out of the closet?" asked an American reporter who hadn't been around for Swain's original outburst.

"In the heat of the moment some players said things they may now regret," Red said. "We have told them where the organization stands. We'll see what happens."

"You keep talking about the organization, Red," I said. "Does that mean that you don't agree with their position on Joe?"

"I am a member of the organization, too," he said.

"Did Ted lay down the law, Red?" asked Bill Sanderson, referring to Ted Ferguson, the team owner.

"What are you trying to get me to say?" said Red, angrily. "That I don't like it? All right. I don't like it. But my feelings about homosexuals have nothing to do with the job we have to do, which is win a pennant. As long as Joe is doing the job on the field, which he is, better than some of the other guys I won't name, I have no beef with him."

"But how can a queer in the clubhouse not affect the team?" asked Keith Jarvis, the weasel from the *Mirror*. "Get real, Red."

"We've won two games since Ms. Henry's story appeared. We're doing all right on the field."

"What are you going to do if the fighting continues?"

"I'm assuming right now that some people might come to their senses when they understand how things stand. If not, we'll have to see."

Several reporters began to shout out questions at once.

"Look, fellahs, I've said all I have to say about the subject. Give me a break. I got a day off, too, and I want to start enjoying it."

Grumbling slightly, they filed out of the room. I hung back. I wanted to talk to the manager about the Japanese player for my sidebar. He had started to strip off his uniform. As his jersey cleared the top of his head, he saw me there.

"For Christ's sake, what are you doing here? Haven't you caused enough trouble? I've got nothing to say to you, hear me? Nothing. Nada. Zip. Sweet fuck-all. So just fuck off before I say what I really mean."

"I don't want to talk about Joe, Red," I sighed. "It's Watanabe. What do you think so far?"

"Too early to tell," he grunted. "I don't think they have the wherewithal to make it in the big leagues. Don't print that. He made a nice play today. We'll have to see if he can hit big-league pitching. Besides, he's so polite he gives me the creeps. Don't print that either."

"I would have thought you would like a player that shows the manager some respect."

"Well, yeah, there is that. But it ain't natural, all his yes sir, no sir, all the time. I'm afraid he's going to bow to me or something. Christ, no one ever told me it was going to be like this. I've got a faggot in left field and a Nip at short and I'm expected to manage them like normal ballplayers."

One leg out of his uniform pants, he stopped and looked at me.

"DON'T PRINT THAT EITHER," he shouted. "And get out of here and let me get my clothes off."

"See you Tuesday," I said. "Have a nice off-day."

I think I heard him growling as I left and went down the hall.

CHAPTER

25

I filed my game story and two short sidebars, about Watanabe and the brawl, from my office at home. When Christopher Morris phoned, I arranged to meet him at The Fillet of Soul, a restaurant specializing in southern cooking. We'd eaten there the last time he was in Toronto, and he told me he'd been dreaming of their ribs and collard greens ever since.

I called Andy and explained that I had a hot date with my sportswriting hero.

"Why don't you join us?"

"And talk baseball all night? No thanks," he said. He sounded weary.

"He can actually talk about other things," I said. "That's why I like him. Come on. It will do you good."

"What time are you meeting him?"

"In an hour. Eight o'clock."

"I'll see what I can do. If I'm not there by eight-thirty, go ahead without me. Maybe I'll join you for a drink afterwards."

"Please try to make it," I said. "You could stand a hearty meal."

"I said I'll see what I can do, okay?"

"You don't have to bite my head off," I said. "I just want to see you. Since when is that an indictable offence?"

"I'm exhausted, Kate. I've been reading computer printouts all day long. The staff inspector is on my back. The FBI is still in town."

"All the more reason to relax and forget about it for a couple of hours. It's Sunday night, for God's sake."

"I'll try, really."

"I know you will. And tomorrow night, Joe and his friend are coming. I'd like it if you could be there."

"If I can, I will. And I'll get there sometime tonight. I promise."

I showered and changed into a pair of slacks and a green silk shirt that matches my eyes. On the way out, I stopped by Sally's. They were having dinner. Elwy was there, too, looking up at me without shame from his own plate of table scraps.

"What a lovely family scene," I said. "Where is David? Off being sincere elsewhere?"

T.C. laughed. Sally didn't. I mentally slapped myself in the face. Sometimes I think I should get a tongue transplant.

"I'm sorry," I said. "I just stopped by to see if you guys can come to supper tomorrow night. Joe's coming, with his friend Sandy."

"Oh boy, can we, Mum? Please."

T.C. had obviously got over his squeamishness about Joe's sexual preferences and was ready to be buddies again.

"Sure. That would be great. Can I bring anything?"

"No, I'm just going to barbecue if the weather stays nice. If not, I'll fake it. Nothing fancy. Six o'clock."

"See you then."

"Drop Fatso upstairs when you're tired of his company. I'm going to the Fillet."

"With anyone we know?" Sally asked.

"I have a date with an older man," I said, then explained about Christopher. "His nibs may or may not join us."

"Have fun."

I decided to take the streetcar on the not-too-remote chance that I might drink enough later to make driving illegal. Also, I hoped I would be coming home with Andy.

I walked out to Broadview Avenue. The King streetcar rattled along almost immediately, practically empty, having begun its journey two blocks away at the Broadview subway station. I settled into a double seat on the right-hand side for the view across the park to the downtown lights, twinkling in the twilight. It's the best view in Toronto. A few elderly Chinese were doing tai-chi exercises at the base of the statue of Sun Yat-sen, watched by a couple of anglo kids leaning on their bicycles. The spring weather had brought Torontonians out of hibernation.

At the corner of Broadview and Gerrard, dozens of Chinese piled into the car, fresh from their shopping at the grocery stores around the intersection with their displays of exotic produce labelled in elegant calligraphy. An elderly lady sat next to me, then turned to talk to her friend in the seat behind. Neither spoke enough English to understand my offer to change places with the friend, but with sign language we got the switch accomplished, then smiled broadly in cross-cultural fellowship.

My new seat mate, a stolid-looking middle-aged man in a suit shiny with wear, opened the *Planet*, turned immediately to the sports section and began to read my story. This has happened to me before, and it always gives me a little charge, a mixture of pride and embarrassment. I'm always tempted to identify myself and ask what they think, but I've never dared. I've also never given in to the temptation to comment on what a fine writer I think the reporter is.

I got to the restaurant a few minutes early, so I joined the owners at the bar. Tom Jefferson came to Toronto in the sixties to play football. In that era, the National Football League didn't believe that blacks had the necessities to quarterback, but the Canadian Football League didn't suffer from that particular bit of mean bigotry. He met and married Sarah and decided to stay after his long and successful career. They opened the restaurant, serving the kind of food Tom had grown up on in Georgia, and it became a second home for visiting athletes, local blacks, and anyone else who loved ribs, fried chicken, black-eyed peas, and jazz on the sound system.

Sarah, blonde and motherly, though not much older than I am, hugged me when I arrived. Tom, behind the bar, shook my hand. I hadn't been in since before spring training, so we spent ten minutes catching up on my news, their news, and gossip about some of the other regulars.

Christopher arrived right on time. Tom and Sarah greeted him like an old friend, despite the fact that he had been there just once before.

"Scotch for you, am I right?" Tom asked.

"Good memory, but I think I'll join Kate in a martini this time."

"Table for two?"

"Andy might be joining us," I said.

Sally led us to a table in the corner.

"Andy? Do I know him?" Christopher asked.

"No, he's not a sportswriter. Just a nice guy I think you might like. Actually, come to think to it, you have met him. I forgot that you were here during the murders last year. Andy, also known as Staff Sergeant Munro, was in charge of the investigation."

"And?"

"And I've been seeing him since then."

I don't know why I was embarrassed to tell Christopher this. There had never been anything between us but mutual admiration and friendship. Christopher is almost a father figure to me, professionally. Perhaps that's why I was anxious for him to like Andy.

"I hope you don't mind that I invited him," I said. "He's in the middle of a tough case and he could use the distraction."

"Not at all. I remember him. Quite a good-looking fellow, I think."

"So do I."

"What's the case?"

"It's pretty nasty. A series of killings of young boys. Also molesting. They call him the Daylight Stalker."

"That's horrible."

I was filling him in on the details when Andy arrived. He had gone home to change and was dressed in nicely fitting jeans and a soft blue sweater. He sat down. Sarah brought our martinis and a coffee for Andy, who was half on duty. We ordered our dinner. Ribs for the men, fried chicken for me, and collard greens all around.

"Kate has been telling me about the murders," Christopher said. "It's a terrible story. It must be very frustrating for you."

"It's not exactly fun," Andy acknowledged.

"It's a fascinating business, serial killing. My brother-in-law is Montague Browning. Have you heard of him?"

"Of course," said Andy, obviously impressed. "I'm a great admirer of his. His book is the best thing written on the subject."

"What is it called?" I asked.

"*Studies in Serial Psychopathology*," said Christopher.

"Snappy title," I said.

"It's not a mass-market book," Christopher said. "He's a professor of forensic psychiatry at Columbia."

"And he is respected by any homicide cop I've ever talked to," Andy added. "What's he like?"

"A very congenial guy," Christopher said. "His specialty makes for some pretty gruesome conversations around the family dinner table, but he is a very cheerful chap. My sister is devoted to him, and he's my youngest son's favourite uncle. But he's at the age when mayhem is particularly fascinating."

"Like T.C. My tenant's kid, who's not quite twelve, thinks Andy is almost as exciting as the baseball players."

"I think we are all secretly like that. I was on a jury for a murder trial a couple of years ago, and I dined out on it for a week. Everybody wanted all the details."

"So do I," I said.

"Just a depressing New York murder. Two neighbours disagreed about a barking dog and one of them ended up dead. The man with the dog just happened to be carrying a revolver in his bathrobe pocket at seven in the morning."

"It's the American Way," I said.

"In his neighbourhood, you'd probably carry a gun, too, Kate," Christopher said. "Try to curb your smug nationalism for a moment."

"Do you carry one?"

"Are you nuts? The things terrify me," he said. "But I live in a building with a doorman and neighbours who are more likely to bore me to death than shoot me."

"I was afraid you guys would spend the whole dinner talking shop about baseball, and you're talking my shop instead," Andy said. "Tell me more about your brother-in-law. I've heard he's revising his book."

"He's finished. It's coming out next month."

"And a year later here, probably."

"I could send you one, if you like."

"I'd appreciate that. Does he deal with the killings in Larchmont?"

"Ah, the Westchester Creeper, as the tabloids called him. Yes. That was a fascinating character, a classic case."

"Who on earth was the Westchester Creeper?" I asked, feeling a tad left out.

"He killed seven children over a period of six months. He was caught with the kid who was to be his eighth victim. I'm interested, because our guy here seems to be behaving in a similar pattern. I've talked to the police involved in it, but I'd be interested in your brother-in-law's opinion."

"Call him. He'd be glad to talk to you. Mention my name. I'll give you his phone number."

"How much like ours was this guy?" I asked.

"The victims were boys about the same age," Andy said. "There were similar patterns of rape, mutilation, and murder. The killer turned out to be a local merchant and boy scout leader. He was married with children of his own and active in the church."

"It was his background that was classic," Christopher said. "He was sickly as a boy, no good at sports. He could never please his macho father and watched him beat his mother most nights. He left home at fourteen to escape, and lived on his wits. He built a good, respectable life for himself."

"He also got involved in the investigation," Andy said. "The local force ignored him because he was always underfoot. But he finally left enough clues that he could be found."

"It caused the department a lot of grief," Christopher said. "The parents of the later victims felt, quite justifiably, from their point of view, that the police had ignored evidence right under their noses."

"Little wonder," I said.

"Not so fast," Andy said. "You're talking about hindsight, here. I have to identify with the police on this one. There is nothing more annoying than an enthusiastic amateur cluttering up the investigation."

"Looking back, they could see it was a cry for help," Christopher said.

"Is that typical of serial killers?"

"Sometimes," Christopher said. "Sometimes they let success make them careless, but there is considerable evidence that they leave clues so that someone will stop them."

"I wish our guy would oblige."

"Well, maybe he has," I said, and started to tell Christopher about the notes. Andy kicked me under the table.

"Ouch! What did you do that for?"

"For blabbing on about things that are supposed to be confidential parts of the investigation."

"Don't be silly," I said. "Christopher isn't going to print anything."

"Of course not," he said. "And if it makes you feel any better, I probably have an alibi for the times of the killings. This is my first trip to Toronto since the playoffs last October."

"Of course," Andy smiled. "I'm sorry. But you will keep this to yourself."

"Right," I said. "So. Hey. Why don't we talk about baseball for a while?"

"Great idea," said Andy.

CHAPTER

26

We all had to work in the morning, so we didn't linger too long over coffee. Tom and Sarah joined us as the restaurant emptied, bringing a round of cognacs with them. It was a lovely, relaxed evening, far away from the problems on the playing field and the children of the city. I was yawning when Andy parked in the driveway.

"Come on, you slug," he said, coming around to open my door and drag me out of the car.

"Tired," I mumbled, leaning on his shoulder.

"Bed," he replied.

Arms around each other, we strolled up the walk. Jim Wells was waiting for us.

"Where the hell have you been?" he asked Andy.

"I left the number with the desk," he said.

"You left a wrong number. We woke up some old lady who subsequently called 911 to say she was getting obscene phone calls."

I giggled, but not for long.

"This concerns you, too, Kate. He left another note."

"What about the goddamn surveillance?" Andy asked. "Didn't our guy see anything?"

"He had gone down the lane to take a leak," Jim said, embarrassed. "He found the note tucked under his windshield wiper when he got back."

"Who was on duty?"

"Larsen."

"He's off the case," Andy said. "Let's see the damn note."

"Let's go inside," Jim said.

Once we were inside my house, he handed Andy a baggie with the note inside. I looked over his shoulder.

It had the same salutation as the last one, my byline clipped from the paper.

"Tell your boyfriend to sleep well tonight," it read. "The stalking is almost over. Four is my lucky number. What is his?"

"Damn," said Andy. "Let's go check your phone."

There were three messages. One, from a former boyfriend inviting me to lunch, was a bit embarrassing to listen to with Andy there. The second was from Sally, saying she would be late for dinner the next night, but that T.C. would be right on time. The third was from Dickie Greaves. God knows what he wanted. I'd see him at the office. Nothing else. No mysterious whispers or heavy breathing.

"Coffee?"

"Sure," said Andy, moving Elwy out of his favourite spot on the couch and sitting down.

"Appreciate it," Jim said. "Can I use your phone to call Carol and tell her I won't be home?"

"Help yourself," I said.

By the time I'd made the coffee and brought it into the living room, the partners were in deep gloom, talked out.

"Well, this is a cheery little group," I said. "Did you tell Jim about our conversation with Christopher? The evening wasn't a complete waste."

Andy told him Christopher's relationship with Montague Browning, the guru of serial death.

"I'm going to call him in the morning, see if he has anything new to tell us. It's very like the Larchmont murders, and he evidently has some new angles on that one."

"Why don't you call him now? You've got his home number," I said.

"It's late."

"Just past eleven. Maybe he stays up late. I'll call Christopher and ask."

"It would beat doing nothing," Jim said.

I went to the kitchen phone.

Christopher said that he didn't think it was too late, and offered to call him first to set it up. I consulted with Andy, then agreed.

We waited five minutes before making the call, Andy and Jim running down the questions they wanted to ask him. They made the call from my study, where they could take notes. They were back in ten minutes.

"He's checking through his computer for us," Andy said. He's going to see if he can find any similarities. He's as well connected as the FBI, only more friendly."

"Maybe another angle will help us out," Jim said. "Sometimes the amateur has a different view on things."

"Ahem," I said.

"Right, Kate," Andy said. "But you're out of this one. I told him to call us back at the office. We'd better get going, Jim."

"You're leaving me here alone?"

"There's still a stakeout across the street. We'll add someone at the back."

"This time, give the guys a bottle to pee in," I said.

I'm fairly brave, but I'm not stupid. Chances are the killer wasn't after me, a grown woman, but if he changed his habits, I didn't want to be the one to start the new trend.

"Don't worry, Kate," Andy said. "They will be there."

"Okay," I said, and got up to see them to the door.

"Thanks for the coffee," Jim said, before discreetly leaving us alone.

"And thanks for the evening, too," Andy said. "It was good to relax. Christopher is a really interesting guy, and it may even turn out to be helpful."

"You don't mean I was right!"

"For once," he said, kissing me on the forehead, a tender but condescending gesture that always pisses me off.

"I don't know when I'll be seeing you. If I can, I'll be here for dinner tomorrow, but it doesn't look good. I think this guy means what he says."

"Be careful," I said, hugging him.

"You too," he said, hugging me back.

I bolted the outside door. There was a crack of light under Sally's door. I tapped on it gently.

"Come on in," she said. "I'm just watching a movie. Is something wrong?"

"No, not really."

I told her about the letter that had just arrived. She shivered.

"I just thought you should know. You'd better put the chain on the door tonight. But don't worry. There are cops all around. I didn't want you to freak if you got up in the night and saw a strange man lurking in the back yard."

"Come have a glass of wine," she said.

"I shouldn't," I said, but followed her into the kitchen.

"I'm really sorry about the remark I made about David, earlier," I said. "I didn't really mean it."

She shrugged.

"You're probably right. It's not working out anyway."

She sat down at the kitchen table.

"I thought it would be good to have a nice, normal guy in my life. And in T.C.'s. But it's not really happening for either of us. T.C. resents him, and he's starting to give me the creeps."

"How so?"

"Put it this way. Maybe he's not a nice, normal guy."

"Are we talking seriously kinky?" I asked.

"Kinky enough that he's history."

"Details, woman."

"Some other time," she said. "Right now, I'm trying to cheer myself up."

She raised her glass towards the living room. She had paused a tape on the VCR. Ginger Rogers, wearing jodhpurs and a plaid jacket, was sitting in a gazebo while the rain poured down outside. Fred Astaire was frozen halfway up the steps in a hansom cab driver's greatcoat, a giant umbrella held rakishly.

"Care to join me?"

"*Top Hat!*" I said. "I can't pass on *Top Hat*! If that won't chase the bogey men away, nothing will."

We took the bottle and glasses and settled in on opposite ends of the couch. Within moments, we were singing along with "Isn't this a lovely day to be caught in the rain?" By the time they were dancing cheek to cheek, Ginger's feathers flying, we had finished the wine and were dancing along, all over the tiny living room.

When I stumbled up the stairs at 1:30, I knew I would have a good night's sleep. Or coma. Whatever, I wasn't going to be tossing and turning.

I put the chain lock on my door and checked to see that my shadow was in place in his car across the street, then went directly to bed.

I was almost asleep when the phone rang.

"Screw you," I said. "I'm not going to let you scare me any more tonight."

The machine picked up after four rings.

CHAPTER

27

Morning came earlier than I wanted, but not as early as it was supposed to. With my mind elsewhere by the time I got to bed, I had forgotten to set the alarm. By the time I came to, it was 9:30. Joe's press conference was called for 11:00. I showered quickly, downed a couple of Tylenols with codeine, and was on my way in twenty minutes, a record of some sort.

There was a scrawled note from Sally tacked to the front door: "See you tonight. Look in on the kid when you get home. He has to do his homework before supper. Thanks, Sal. P.S. I don't feel so much like dancing this A.M."

I was feeling a bit frail myself. I banged myself on the shin opening the garage door and tripped over a rake.

But it was a beautiful day. My barbecue idea was a go. I rolled back the top on the Citroën to catch some early rays and clear my head. I wanted to stop in at the office on the way. If I picked up my mail and checked my messages, maybe I could avoid going in later. Besides, the cafeteria made a decent cup of coffee, which I could use.

I grabbed one on the way up, then spilled some on my skirt. This wasn't my day, obviously.

The sports department was all but deserted. I dumped my stuff and went to the ladies' room to wet a towel and rub out the stain. I stood at my desk so my skirt would dry without wrinkling. There was an inch-high stack of pink message slips, mostly from baseball reporters around the league wanting the dirt on Joe. Nothing urgent. I stuck them in my briefcase and went through the mail. Press releases and other crap. Right at the bottom of the pile, though, was a strange one. Strange, but familiar.

I picked up the phone and dialled Andy's number.

"I got another one at the office, Andy. Do you want me to open it?"

"When did it come in?"

"I don't know. I haven't cleaned out my mailbox since at least Thursday. Maybe even before that."

"Is there a stamp? Did it go through the mail?"

"I don't know. There's a stamp, but no postmark. Either it was delivered by hand or they screwed up at the post office for a really big change."

"Open it, but carefully."

Inside was a two-word message, in banner head-line type: "STOP ME."

"I'll send someone right over."

"I won't be here. I have to go to the press conference. I'll leave it with Jake Watson."

"The editor? Okay."

"How are you? Have you had any sleep since you left my place?"

"A couple of hours on a couch here. I feel like shit."

"Poor baby. Why don't you go home and have a shower and change your clothes?"

"Too much to do."

"Is there anything new?"

"Well, Browning found four similar-pattern series of murders. One of them is Canadian."

"Really? Where?"

"It happened in Timmins about three years ago. There were just two kids killed, six months apart. The police there weren't positive they were connected. But Browning had them in his files as a possible. I have a call in to the police chief up there."

"What were the other cases?"

"There were three kids murdered in upstate New York a few years ago, and others in Colorado and suburban Chicago. I've got the FBI guys on those."

"Do you think there might be some connection?"

"I don't know. But we have to chase any possibility, no matter how slim."

"Maybe something will come out of it," I said. "Any chance you'll be by tonight?"

"Depends on how it goes, but I doubt it."

"Okay. I'll see you when I see you."

"Bye."

Poor guy. I checked my watch and grabbed my notebook, computer, and briefcase. I put the letter from the creep in an envelope with Andy's name on it and stuck it on Jake's desk with an explanatory note. Then I ran into him as he was getting off the elevator.

"Aren't you supposed to be at a press conference?"

"I'm on my way. I've left something on your desk. The cops will be by to pick it up. If you're not here, make sure someone knows about it."

"Is it a mash note or are you playing Nancy Drew again?"

"Not of my free will," I said, then hit the button for the lobby.

"What will you have for me today?"

The door started to close. I stopped it with my arm.

"It depends on what happens at the press conference. Probably not much. Have you got anyone else on it?"

The elevator began to buzz at me.

"Jeff wants to write a column on him," Jake said. "And the folks upstairs want a takeout on homos in sport. Interested?"

"Not particularly, but I'll do it if you want me to."

"I'll try to get someone else on it. It just needs a bunch of phone calls. I'd rather you stuck with Kelsey."

"I'll call in after the conference. I'll probably be writing from home."

"Fine."

The door slid shut. When it opened on the next floor down, six people glared at me and crowded on.

"Lovely day," I said.

CHAPTER

28

The Titans had set up an interview room in the visiting clubhouse for Joe's press conference. There were cameras from the two Canadian networks, the cable sports channel, and several local stations. The American nets were there, too. In front of the camera stand were a dozen rows of chairs, mostly full. Some reporters were sitting on the players' stools in front of the lockers. There were a dozen microphones taped to a stand at the front of the room.

I found a seat next to Christopher Morris.

"Thanks for calling your brother-in-law," I said.

"He was glad to help," he said. "Did he?"

"Did he what?"

"Help?"

"I think so. But, as you saw last night, I'm not supposed to talk about anything."

"Right," he said, smiling. "I liked your Andy, by the way. Unusual for a cop."

"He liked you, too."

The door opened, and Joe Kelsey walked in, accompanied by an uncomfortable-looking Hugh Marsh and a third man I recognized as his agent, Peter Moir.

"Can I have your attention please, gentlemen, and Kate," Marsh said, looking around the room. "Joe Kelsey is here to answer any questions you might have, but first he has a brief statement. Joe."

Nothing Joe was saying was new to me. I watched the room for reaction. The reporters looked uncomfortable. Most of them have so completely bought into jock myths that they are as conservative as the fellows they cover. There was hostility in the room, both because of Joe's homosexuality and because of the way they were being forced to cover it. Sportswriters, especially heavy hitters like some of the ones in the room, don't like sharing their interviews with others. The columnist from the New York *Times* led off.

"Why did you come out? Couldn't you just go on the way you've been and save everybody a lot of pain?"

"I have to think about my own pain," Joe said. "If I am no longer ashamed of being gay, why should I hide it? With all respect, it's not my problem any more."

"But surely you knew what this would do to baseball?"

"Last time I checked, baseball was the same game it's been for one hundred years. It takes more than something like this to change that."

"Do you know of any other gay ballplayers?" asked a guy from the New York *Post*.

"No, I don't."

"Do you think you're the only one?"

"I doubt it."

"Would you urge them to follow your example?"

"That's not for me to do. I imagine there might be some people right now waiting to see what happens to me."

The man from *Sports Illustrated* interrupted the line of questioning impatiently.

"You've put your team-mates in a difficult position by asking them to accept you. Baseball is based on team play, on the chemistry among the players. How is this going to affect the Titans?"

"If we can have Dominican players and black players and redneck players and even a Japanese player on the same team and keep on winning, I don't see what difference I'm going to make. And in case you haven't noticed, I'm having the best start of my career. I don't see how that is going to hurt the team."

"That fight in the locker room yesterday after the game wasn't exactly team spirit at its best, Joe," said one of the writers from Detroit.

"I'll let you in on a secret," Joe smiled. "Stinger and me didn't exactly get along before last week, either. So our relationship hasn't changed because I'm gay."

He was magnificent. He never lost his temper and never let them make him feel like a freak. Every challenge the reporters threw at him, he threw right back. The overall message implicit, though never stated, was that any problem his homosexuality was causing was the bigots' fault, not Joe's.

The press conference lasted for an hour. Afterwards, Joe was mobbed by reporters looking for their own angles and cameras trying to get an exclusive shot. He patiently answered questions for another half hour.

There wasn't much of a story for me. A mood piece. I hit up a couple of the high-profile American reporters for their thoughts, and grabbed Joe on the way out the door for a few quotes on the reaction so far.

"It hasn't been as bad as I thought it would be," he said. "The fans have been very accepting, and most of my team-mates have been all right."

"Except for Stinger."

"You know that's not the first time we've mixed it up. And it won't be the last time, but not getting along hasn't stopped us from playing winning base-ball together."

"Thanks, Joe, I'll see you later. I should be finished early. Why don't you guys come by at about four? We can sit in the garden. And besides, that means T.C. won't be bugging me every five minutes about when you're going to get there."

"Sure. It will be nice to be somewhere quiet. These guys are still outside my place all the time."

"Just don't let them follow you to my place."

"No worry. I watch *Magnum P.I.* every afternoon. I can shake a tail."

"As the actress said to the bishop."

"Pardon?"

"Never mind, Joe. The joke is older than you are. I'll see you at four."

CHAPTER

29

I stopped at the supermarket on the Danforth on the way home and picked up a couple of dozen shishkebabs, already assembled and marinated, for dinner. I didn't know how many I would be feeding or how big their appetites might be. I could always freeze the leftovers. I got garlic tzatziki at Alex Farms, salad stuff at Sunland, and buns at the corner store. It was just a typical lazy person's Danforth meal, but I hoped it might seem more exotic to Joe and Sandy. Then I hit the liquor store for red wine and the beer store for a dozen.

I was home just before 2:00. I unpacked the groceries, mixed some red wine, garlic, hot sauce, and olive oil and set the kebabs in to soak. I changed into jeans, then made myself a peanut butter and jelly sandwich and ate it in front of my computer in the study, going through my notes and figuring out what to say about the morning's session.

I got the story done and filed by 3:30, then lay down for a recuperative catnap. Literally. Elwy lay purring on my chest, to make sure I didn't really fall asleep. I got up after forty-five minutes, feeling only marginally better, threw cold water on my face, then went to the garage to dig out the barbecue stuff. I left a note for Joe and Sandy on the front door, telling them to come around the back.

The barbecue was in the garage, covered with a winter's worth of dust. To my horror, but not surprise, I discovered that I hadn't bothered to clean the grill after my last cookout. I was just dusting off the outdoor furniture when they arrived. Joe had flowers, Sandy a bottle of good California wine.

"What wonderful guests," I said. "Here, sit down and let me get you something. Shall I open the wine, or do you want a real drink?"

"Just a beer for me," Sandy said.

"Me too," said Joe.

"I'll be right back," I said.

Sandy came up the back stairs to the kitchen while I was arranging the flowers in an old cranberry-glass pitcher that had belonged to my grandmother.

"That looks nice. It's a beautiful vase."

I thanked him and put it on the kitchen table and went to the fridge.

"How is he?" I asked. "And how are you, too? Sorry."

"We're fine," Sandy said. "A little shaky, but strong, too. How do you think it went this morning?"

"He was really terrific."

"He told me he did all right," laughed Sandy.

200

"Joe has never been known for overstating things. He was superb."

"I'm glad."

"Me too."

I gave him the tray with the beers and followed him down the stairs.

"So, where is T.C.?" Joe asked. "I thought he would be here."

"Oh, Christ. I forgot I was supposed to look in on him," I said. I went to the downstairs back door and pounded on it. There was no reponse.

"Maybe he's changed his mind about wanting to see me," Joe said. "I wouldn't blame him."

"Don't be an asshole," I said. "He is an extremely liberated young fellow. If he wasn't, Sally and I would wring his neck. It's just that he wasn't expecting you until later. He's probably just stopped off to play catch."

I rolled out the hose and wet down the grill, sprinkled it with cleanser, and got the wire brush. Joe jumped up and took it from my hand.

"Let me do it," he said. "This was my job at home."

"Are you any good?"

"At barbecue cleaning, I'm an all-star. My mama made sure of that."

The phone rang. I ran up the stairs to catch it before the fourth ring, when the answering machine usually takes over, but it just rang twice. I tripped over the door-sill and swore, then grabbed the receiver. I could hear my voice droning on, and shouted over it to the person on the other end. After the beep, I could hear Sally laughing.

"Get it together, woman," she said.

"The machine kicked in early. There must be a message. What's up?"

"Nothing. I want to talk to my son."

"He's not here yet."

"Are you sure? He's not at home, either. He's usually there by three-thirty."

"It's not much after four. Not to worry. I'll have him call you as soon as he gets in."

"I'm going out myself in half an hour to meet with a big bucks Rosedale client. I should be home by six-thirty, seven at the latest."

"See you then. I hope you'll be fat with commissions. I'll have T.C. call if he gets here in the next little while. If he doesn't, I'll give him shit for you."

I went to my study to check the machine, which was still rewinding from my conversation with Sally. There were three messages, in all.

Probably one was from T.C.

The first one wasn't. At first all I heard was breathing. I suddenly remembered the phone call I had ignored when I went to bed. The breathing turned to sobs, then the familiar husky whisper.

"Oh, God, Kate. Help me. Stop me. Don't let me do it again."

I stopped the machine. There was something about the voice, something I recognized behind the disguise. The message ran a second time. I still couldn't quite place it. I let the machine run on past the beep, which was followed by T.C.'s cheery, excited voice.

"Hi, Kate. I'm just reporting in, like the absolutely perfect, well-behaved kid I am. I'll be a little late getting home. I have practice, then I'm going to meet Mr. Greaves at the park at four-thirty. They need to take another picture. I'll be home around five. See you later, alligator."

The realization hit me like a fist in the stomach. I doubled over and screamed. In the background, the tape rolled on, replaying my conversation with Sally: "He's not here yet . . . Are you sure? He's not at home, either . . . It's not much after four. Not to worry. I'll have him call you . . ."

In my head was another conversation, from lunch on Friday: "I'd forgotten you worked in Timmins . . ." And: "This killer is smart. He'll find a way."

I was screaming and swearing incoherently. Joe and Sandy came running. Sandy grabbed me and shook the hysteria out of me.

"What is it?"

T.C. . . . I know who the murderer is . . . we have to get to the park . . . which park? . . . Oh, my God. Oh shit, fuck. . ."

I grabbed the phone, and dialled Andy's number. He wasn't there. Neither was Jim.

"Can I take a message?"

"No, there's not time. You've got to find them. And send some cops to Riverdale Park and Withrow Park fast. I'm not sure which one, but the murderer has got T.C. in one of them."

We wasted minutes in explanations before the poor guy on the other end of the phone made sense of what I was saying. It wasn't his fault. I wasn't making much sense either.

"You stay right there, Ma'am. We'll have an officer with you in a minute."

"I'm not staying anywhere. I'm going to find him. This is all my fault. I should have realized. I have to stop him. He'll listen to me. I know I can stop him. Just get those cops there fast."

"Leave it to us. There's nothing you can do except stay where you are."

"Want to bet?"

I hung up the phone and turned to Joe and Sandy.

"Do you have your car?"

"Yes."

"Let's go. We've got to find him."

The three of us raced down the stairs and got into the ludicrously small car a local Honda dealership supplied to all the players. I made Sandy jam in the back so I could hang out the window and look for T.C. and the man who wanted to kill him. I explained what I thought was happening and directed Joe to Broadview, then told him to drive slowly in the curb lane south past Riverdale Park. I had him stop the car just past the tennis courts while I got out to look down the hill towards the softball diamonds and running track.

"Damn, why didn't I bring my binoculars!"

Joe joined me on the sidewalk.

"There must be a hundred kids down there," he said. "Do you want to go down and look?"

"If he's not there, we haven't got time."

"I'll go. I can run better than you."

"We'll meet you at the bottom of the park."

He took off down the hill faster than he ever beat out an infield hit. He zig-zagged through the groups of children, some of whom recognized him and began to chase after him.

204

I got back into the car on the driver's side.

"What does T.C. look like?" asked Sandy, who had pushed the seat forward and was kneeling on the back with his head out the passenger window.

"He's blond, with glasses. He'll have a baseball glove with him, and probably a cap. Can you see Joe?"

"Yeah, he's still running. What about the guy you think is the murderer?"

"He's medium height, brown hair, good-looking. He'll be wearing a suit or sports jacket. Do you see anything?"

"Nothing. Joe's almost at the bottom of the park. Let's go get him."

I drove. When we got to him, he was out of breath. A gaggle of excited children surrounded him. He jumped into the passenger's seat.

"Sorry, kids, I've got to go," he called to them as I pulled away from the curb. "I'll catch you later."

I did a U-turn back up Broadview, turned right on Riverdale, tires squealing, then gunned through the 40 k/ph zone, past the closely spaced brick houses with their tiny lawns, keeping an eye out for kids, dogs, and cats. Pausing for a nanosecond at the stop sign, I turned left up Logan, by Withrow Park.

Ordinarily the park is one of my favourite spots. It's a lovely place, a hilly park with ball diamonds, playgrounds, trees for strolling under, benches for conversations, a soccer field, and a hockey rink spread out on different levels over an area five blocks long and two blocks across. But this time it seemed full of menace, with too many places to hide.

I drove slowly north, past the lower ball diamond. Nothing. Nothing in the kids' playground or the tennis court. Right on McConnell across the top of the park, past the Greeks arguing on park benches, then right again down Carlaw. He wasn't at the skating rink or on the soccer field. I saw a small figure wearing a Titan's cap sitting on the bleachers at the far side and my heart leaped with hope for a minute, but he turned his head and I saw it wasn't T.C.

"Damn. Damn."

I pounded the steering wheel in frustration, then turned right on Withrow, then right again at Logan for one more pass around.

"What other park could it be? It's got to be some-where nearby. Think, Kate, think."

Joe grabbed my arm.

"Kate, look. There he is."

CHAPTER

30

I stopped the car so suddenly it stalled. I looked where Joe was pointing, over behind the brick changing-house by the skating rink in the middle of the park. No wonder I'd missed him the first time around. T.C. was talking and tossing a ball in the air and catching it over and over. He seemed relaxed. Dickie was leaning against the wall of the building with his arms crossed.

"It doesn't look that dangerous to me," Sandy said.

"Maybe I'm wrong," I said, opening the car door. "But I don't think I am."

"No, Kate, don't get out here," said Joe. "If you're right, we don't want to come busting in there and scare him. Let's just park the car and walk over there, casual like."

He was right. I started the engine again and went up and parked around the corner on Hogarth.

Then the three of us got out and crossed the street into the park.

"I'll wait here in case the cops come," Sandy said.

"Good idea."

Talking calmly, but with every nerve-end tingling, Joe and I strolled over the hill. As we got close, Dickie saw us. He waved and spoke to T.C., who turned around. His face lit up when he saw Joe. We crossed the intervening lawn as quickly as we could while still seeming casual.

"Hi, Kate. Hi, Joe," T.C. said. He looked a bit dozy. There was a Coke can on the grass. Had he been drugged?

"You are in big trouble, kiddo," I said, smiling as best I could. "You were supposed to be home at three-thirty, and your mum's looking for you. So I'd better get you home right now."

"Aw, Kate, we're just waiting for the photographer. It will just take a minute, won't it, Mr. Greaves?"

"Hi, Kate," said my colleague. "Sorry about this, but what's the sweat? The pictures I took on Saturday were no good, so we have to reshoot. Bill Spencer was supposed to be here half an hour ago. He probably got lost or had to go shoot a fire or something."

"That's your problem, I'm afraid," I said, lightly. "T.C.'s problem is that he has to call his mum."

"I did call, honest. Didn't you get my message?"

"I know, T.C. That's how I knew where to find you," I said, and began to edge towards them, keeping my eyes locked with Greaves's.

"And I got your message, too, Dickie. The one from last night. I only picked it up just now."

"What message?"

He looked nervous enough to remove any doubt from my mind. I kept looking into his eyes. For what? Madness? Murderous rage? I saw nothing but his usual bland boyishness, but kept moving slowly towards T.C., who looked confused.

"How can I help you?" I asked.

That was a mistake. Dickie suddenly grabbed T.C. and pulled a knife out of his jacket pocket. He held it to the boy's throat.

"No, Dickie, don't," I said, trying to stay calm. "You don't want to hurt anyone else. We can get you help."

"Don't call me Dickie!" he shouted.

"I'm sorry, Richard," I said. "I didn't know it bothered you."

"Well, it does," he said, quietly, smiling. Now I could see the madness. He began to back away, pulling T.C. with him.

"Don't," I said. "Please. Don't hurt T.C. Please let him go." I tried to ignore the tears sliding down my cheeks.

"If I let him go, you'll sic your big friend on me," Dickie said. "I wouldn't have a chance."

"You want a hostage? Take me instead. Let him go."

Joe put his hand on my arm, as if to restrain me, and gave it a squeeze of warning. Then I saw Sandy, coming slowly around the corner of the changing house, behind Dickie and to his right. I immediately looked back at Dickie so he wouldn't be suspicious. At the same time, I heard sirens on Logan. Dickie looked to his left, towards the street. At that moment Sandy jumped him, knocked T.C. to the ground and grabbed the knife.

Dickie took off across the park towards Carlaw. Joe ran after him and caught up to him at the soccer field, in the middle of a group of children. He tackled him. They wrestled on the ground while the children watched. Dickie never had a chance.

I knelt next to T.C., who was shaking, and held him tight. Suddenly there were uniforms wherever I looked.

"All right, it's over now. You're safe," I said.

I hugged him, then we sat on the grass and watched half a dozen policemen escort Dickie, none too gently, to a cruiser. As they were shoving him into the back seat, he looked over the shoulder of one of the cops and shouted to me.

"Front page, Kate! Above the fold!"

I shuddered and held T.C. a bit closer. Andy found us a few minutes later. He stood a few feet away with his coat open, hands on his hips. I couldn't read his expression.

"What the hell took you so long?" I said, my voice shaking with either relief or anger.

"We were out looking for Greaves," he said. "The police chief in Timmins told me that he had been a suspect in the killings there."

"You were almost too late," I said.

"No thanks to you," he replied.

"No thanks to me? What the hell is that supposed to mean?"

"I mean that you and your goddamned meddling almost got T.C. killed."

"I'm going to ignore that last remark," I said, speaking very carefully. "I think we had better get

T.C. to the hospital in case he was drugged. Did you drink out of that Coke can, T.C.?"

"Yeah," he said. "But I don't get it. Do you really think he's the Daylight Stalker?"

"It looks that way," I said.

"But he seemed like a really nice guy," T.C. said, stifling a yawn.

Joe and Sandy joined us.

"Are you all right, T.C.?" Joe asked. "Kate?"

We stood up.

"We're fine, Preacher," I said. "That was some tackle."

"Just call me Bo Jackson. I'm a two-sport man now."

"Sandy, what you did took guts."

He put one hand on his hip in a camp gesture.

"I may be gay, honey, but I'm no sissy," he said.

Laughter was a relief. He continued in a more serious tone.

"When I saw him pull the knife, I figured I had to risk sneaking up behind him, try to take him by surprise."

"Can you get T.C. to the hospital?" Andy asked. "I'll come over and interview him later."

"Fine." I said, calmly.

"No problem," Joe said. "We'll drive you."

"I'll send a constable along," Andy said. "That way you won't have to wait at Emergency."

He motioned to one of the uniformed cops, who ran over.

"There's no need for you guys to come, really," I said. "Take the key to my place and I'll join you there as soon as I can."

"What, and miss out on this part of the adventure? Forget it," Sandy said. "Besides, I've always wanted to have a police escort."

Our two-car convoy, with flashing lights and a siren, sped across the viaduct and down Sherbourne. I rode in the back of the cruiser with T.C., who was groggy but babbling with excitement. I wasn't listening. I was thinking about Andy's anger.

Once we got to the Wellesley Hospital, T.C. was taken immediately to an examining room. Sandy, Joe, and I stayed in the waiting room, surrounded by the walking wounded in various states of pain or boredom. We weren't lonely. Other patients recognized Joe and he was kept busy signing autographs. The whole scene became quite surreal. We were half in shock, I guess. I tried to reach Sally, but there was no answer at the gallery.

T.C. wasn't long. He came out looking more alert, but faintly green.

"They made me puke," he said. "Yuck."

The nurse handed a bag to the constable. He looked at it dubiously.

"You'll want to have it analyzed," she explained.

The young cop took it.

"Make sure you don't get it confused with your lunch," Sandy said. The forced humour was just what was needed. It made me laugh, anyway, and T.C. looked appropriately grossed out.

"Can we go now, Kate?" he asked.

"Sure, if that's all right with you, officer."

"I'll escort you back," he said.

"There's no need," I said.

"Kate, come on! I want the sirens again," said T.C.

212

"Don't be a goof. The man has evidence to deliver."

"Sure, you wouldn't want to hold up the puke patrol," said Sandy.

"The retch run," I said.

"The barf battalion," chimed in T.C., giggling.

"You guys are making me sick," Joe said.

As we headed out of the hospital, T.C. asked where his mother was.

"She's at a meeting. I couldn't reach her. We'll see her at home. I don't know how I'm going to explain this one. Some baby-sitter I am!"

"Well, you did save his life," Joe said.

"Thanks to you guys," I said.

"Kate?"

"Yes, T.C."

"What's for dinner? I'm starved."

Joe and I exchanged looks over the kid's head. I shrugged.

CHAPTER

31

"Are you sure you're all right?" I asked T.C. We were in the back of Joe's Honda, on the way home.

"Why not? He didn't hurt me," he said. "Wait until I tell the kids at school! I survived the Daylight Stalker!"

"That wasn't a movie, T.C. It really happened. You were really in danger," I said.

"I know," he shrugged. "But I'm okay, so what's the big deal?"

"You're weird," I said.

"I know," he laughed.

I hugged him, to reassure myself as much as anything. T.C. was doing just fine. I knew the crash would come, but if he wanted to play it cool for the moment, who was I to argue?

Who indeed? Just someone who had sat next to a serial killer at work for the past two years. Just somebody who hadn't noticed a thing strange about a man who could rape and murder little children. I shuddered.

Joe and Sandy were quiet in the front seat, taking their lead from me.

"I'd better call the paper," I said as we pulled into the driveway.

"I'll take care of the barbecue," Joe said.

"And, if you don't mind, I'll open some wine," Sandy said. "I think we all could use some."

I called the sports department first. I thought I had better tell Jake that one of his staff had just been arrested. He wasn't there. Rather than explain it all to the night editor, I tried Jake's home number. No answer. I looked up the number of The Final Edition. Lenore found him for me.

"Oh, Jesus," was all he said, when I told him.

"I don't know what you want to do about it. Pull his story from tomorrow's paper, for one thing. I haven't told anyone upstairs yet. I thought you'd like to do that. If they haven't got it off the police radio."

"Oh, Jesus," he said again.

"You'll have to figure out what you want from me, if anything. Or maybe the city desk will. I'll leave it to you. When it has sunk in, give me a call. I'm at home. Kelsey and his friend are here, too."

"You're sure T.C. is all right?"

"He's fine," I said. "Pretty excited, as a matter of fact. The nightmares will come later."

"Mine have just begun. I'll get upstairs now and figure out how the hell to handle this. I'll call you back when I've figured it out. Dickie Greaves. Jesus."

"I know. Talk to you later," I said.

I tried Andy, but he couldn't come to the phone.

Just as well, probably. I didn't much feel like dealing with his attitude. On the other hand, I could use some support, if he could stand offering it. Particularly when Sally got home.

I went down the back stairs to the garden. T.C. was helping Joe with the barbecue. Sandy was sitting at the picnic table. He had found the wine cooler and glasses, and was sipping thoughtfully while he watched his lover and the boy whose life they had saved. I sat down on the bench next to him. He poured me a glass of wine and handed it to me. Then he covered my hand with his and squeezed it.

"It's all over," he said.

It was strange, but we all behaved quite calmly, as if the terrifying scene in the park had been nothing more than a minor interruption of our dinner party, as if it had happened to someone else.

So it was quite a normal scene that greeted Sally when she came through the back door of her ground floor flat. Joe and T.C. were hosing out the barbecue, laughing and getting wet. Sandy and I were giving helpful advice from our dry spot.

"What a day," Sally said, dropping into a deck chair. "I am pooped. And you, you little creep, you didn't call me."

"Let me pour you a glass of wine," I said, quickly.

"Hey, you guys probably haven't heard the good news," Sally said. "I just heard a bulletin on the car radio. They think they've got the Stalker."

Glances were exchanged, but no one said a word. My job, I guess. I handed her the glass and took a deep breath. Why did I feel guilty?

"We do know about it, as a matter of fact," I

began. "I'm not sure how to tell you this, but we were there when they caught him."

"You were *what*?"

"Now, don't panic. Just listen."

"They saved my life, Mum," T.C. said. "Joe and Sandy. And Kate."

"Why do I get the feeling I'm about to scream?" she asked. T.C. went and leaned against her chair.

"You'd have every right to," I said, laughing nervously. "But you don't have to. It's over. Everything is all right. It's just that . . ."

Christ, how to put it? Straight, I guess.

"It's just that T.C. was next on his list."

"And they made me puke at the hospital," T.C. said. "I was practically killed."

"Thanks, T.C., you're a big help," I said.

"Will somebody please tell me what happened," Sally said, her voice very controlled.

So I did, giving her the basic facts as quickly as I could. She reached out and put her arms around T.C., her head against his chest, her face suddenly pale. When she looked up, tears stood in her eyes.

"Oh, God, thank you. Thank you all very, very much. Without my son, I don't know . . ."

"Aw, Mum, don't get all mushy," T.C. said, breaking the tension. All the grownups were laughing and crying at the same time. Sally stood up and hugged me, then Joe.

"We haven't met, yet," she said to Sandy. "I'm Sally Parkes and I would like very much to hug you, too."

He put his arms out, she stepped into them, and he held her close.

"All right," she said finally, wiping tears from her eyes. "Now I want to hear all about it from you, T.C."

"He came to the school at lunch hour. I was in the playground. He told me that the picture they took on Saturday didn't turn out and I should meet him at the park at four. He told me not to tell any of the other kids, because they would be jealous." He shrugged. "I didn't think there was anything wrong. You let me go with him before, and he was a friend of Kate's."

Sally and I exchanged a look, part guilt, part horror.

"I called Kate and left a message on her machine after school," T.C. continued, somewhat defensively.

"Which I forgot to check when I came in," I explained. "I didn't realize that there were any messages until you called."

"So I went there, to the park," T.C. continued. "He got there a little bit later and told me we had to wait for the photographer. He bought me a Coke."

"Which will probably turn out to have been drugged," I said.

"Which is why they made me puke at the hospital. Yuck."

"What did he say?" Sally asked. "What did you talk about?"

"Just stuff. About baseball and about the other kids he'd written stories about. And about when he was a kid and nobody ever picked him for the team. Like me, until they found out I could pitch. He was really nice."

"Weren't you scared?"

"No, why should I be scared? We were just talking. I didn't know what was happening until it was over."

"Did he suggest you go anywhere else?"

"Well, he said that if the guy didn't get there soon, he would give me a ride home in his van."

The van, one of the things that should have tipped me off sooner. I interrupted and filled her in on my half of the story.

"After I talked to you, I checked my machine. T.C.'s wasn't the only message. Dickie had left one, too, only I didn't know it was Dickie. It was late last night and I didn't bother to answer the phone. This morning I was late and hungover and forgot all about the call.

"It was like the one he left before. He was asking me to help him. Something just twigged. The way he spoke, I realized that he knew me. That he knew who he was talking to. And I thought I recognized the voice."

"How could you be sure?" Sally asked.

"I couldn't. But I couldn't take a chance. There was something else, too. Andy told me this morning that this expert had told him about some similar murders in Timmins. I remembered that Dickie had worked in Timmins for a while. And I thought about the way he has been fascinated by the murders, and how he talked about the killer. He said he was smart. He said something about how he had almost been gentle. It all fit."

I told the story of the chase around the neighbourhood, Sandy and Joe's heroics, Dickie's arrest, and the trip to the hospital.

"What happens now?" Sally asked.

"Andy said he would come and talk to us as soon as they got Dickie put away. I guess we will have to tell the story again."

"Joe and I can get out of here, if you like, Kate," Sandy said. "Would you three rather be alone?"

I looked at Sally, who shook her head.

"No. I'll start dinner," I said. "If you don't mind a bit of confusion, you're welcome to stay."

"I'll be glad to help," Sandy said.

"We're having shishkebabs. I can put them on as soon as the coals are ready. They won't take long."

"Maybe I'll just put on a hot dog for T.C.," Sally said. "It will be quicker."

"I'll go up and start getting the rest of it together," I said.

"I'll come with you," Sandy said, "I am a master salad chef."

"And T.C. and I will start the fire," said Joe.

"After that, do you want to play catch?" T.C. asked.

CHAPTER

32

Sandy turned out to be true to his word. While I prepared some potatoes to roast with garlic, he tore and washed the greens, sliced onions, peppers, and mushrooms, then made a delicious dressing, with my tasting assistance.

My preparations were interrupted by a phone call from the paper. The front page wanted me to dictate an eyewitness story to the rewrite desk.

"I'll call you back in five minutes," I said.

I explained to Sandy what was left to do to the potatoes, then went to my study to collect my thoughts. I decided it was easier to write the story than to dictate it. I think better with my fingers than my mouth. My portable computer was already set up. I wrote a short story, mentioning Joe's role in the capture. I had to be careful that I only wrote what I had seen, not anything I knew because of my conversations with Andy. I transmitted it over the phone to the office computer, then called Jake.

"You should have something in now. Do you want to check?"

"Yeah, it's here," he said, a few minutes later. "I'll get it over to the news desk."

"What's going on down there?"

"What do you think? A staffer is charged with the most horrible crimes the city has ever seen. The city editor has come in to stage-manage the coverage. We can't ignore it, but it's not something we can really run with, under the circumstances."

"For the first time in the history of the *Planet*, you're hoping there's a publication ban soon."

"You got it."

"You have to say something."

"Well, he's innocent until proven guilty. Right now, the news side is more worried about covering our asses than anything else. That's from the publisher on down."

"I don't envy you," I said.

"I don't have to worry about the coverage, but I hired the guy, for Christ's sake."

"No one could have known, Jake."

"Yeah, I guess. What are you going to do tomorrow? Are you all right to go to Detroit, or do you have to stick around to give evidence or something?"

"I'll be doing that later tonight. I'll be ready to go tomorrow. The charter doesn't leave until noon. If I have to, I'll take a later flight."

"I can send someone else if you like."

"No, I'd rather get out of here."

"All right. Let me know what's happening."

"I'll call you in the morning."

I went back to the garden and told Joe what I had written.

222

"I mentioned your name, too, Sandy," I said, hesitantly. "I described you as a friend of Joe's. I hope that's not a problem."

"It's the truth," he said.

"This might take some of the heat off you, Joe," Sally said. "You're a real hero now."

"It was no big deal," he shrugged. "He was just a little guy."

"Big enough," I said.

"What will happen to him?" T.C. asked.

"If he's found guilty, I don't guess he'll ever ever get out of jail," I said.

"Not if I can help it," said Andy, who had overheard us as he came into the yard, along with a uniformed constable. A very attractive female constable, in fact, with blonde hair and dimples. He went immediately to Sally and hugged her. I hung back, waiting for his move.

"Are you all right?" he asked, a little stiffly.

"Fine. I'm just appalled that I didn't figure it out sooner."

"How do you think I feel? It's my job, not yours."

"Do we know for sure?"

"He's the one, all right."

"Did he confess?"

"Not yet. But he will. His kind always does, eventually."

"I sat at the desk next to him for a year," I said. "I can't believe I didn't notice something about him."

"It's always that way," Sandy said. "Whenever something like this happens, don't all the neighbours say what a quiet person the murderer was? It's weird."

"I know it's the great cliché, but I always figured

those neighbours were either really stupid or didn't know the killer well," I said. "But I *knew* Dickie. I had lunch with him. We had beers after work. He was just a normal guy. A bit of an asshole, sometimes, but I had no clue."

"Don't beat yourself up about it, Kate," Andy said. "There's no way you could have known. That's one of the most frightening things about serial killers. Because they really don't believe what they are doing is wrong, it doesn't affect them. They can kill, then go about their business."

"But Dickie couldn't, could he?" I asked. "He wanted to get caught. He laid it all out for me. He was pleading for my help."

"And gave you good reason to catch him by threatening T.C., too," Andy agreed. "It happens that way sometimes. It's as if there is a more rational half of the personality trying to gain control."

"What would have happened if I hadn't figured it out?"

"He would have killed T.C.," Andy said. "To punish you for not being as smart as you thought. I don't think your friend Dickie was too fond of you."

"Jesus," I said.

"Yeah," Andy said. "T.C., are you ready to talk to me? I don't want to take you away from your dinner."

"I'm finished," he said, getting up from the table.

"Can we talk inside?" Andy asked Sally.

"Sure. Shall I come?"

"If you like. And I would really appreciate a coffee, if you could manage it."

"Do you want something to eat?" I asked Andy. "I'm just about to cook."

"No. I had a sandwich. I have to get statements

from you and Joe and Sandy, too. Then I have to get back to the office. I've left your friend with Jim."

"Don't call him my friend, please," I said.

"Sorry. Let's go, T.C."

It didn't take long, but by the time he came back, we were all a little drunk. Screaming tension and three bottles of wine will do that every time. Sandy was telling stories about Joe's first days at the health club, and we were laughing until the tears ran down our faces.

Andy looked at the dirty dishes and empty wine bottles with dismay.

"Great interviews I'm going to have here," Andy said, more grumpily than I thought completely justified.

"No, it's fine," I said. "Don't get your drawers in a knot. Do you want to talk to us separately or together?"

"One at a time," he said. "Joe first. Do you mind if I use your place, Kate? Sally is getting T.C. to bed."

"No problem. You know your way."

It took an hour for us to all tell our stories. The constable left at 9:00, and Joe and Sandy shortly afterwards.

They didn't take the car. Nothing like having a cop in residence to change one's mind about driving drunk.

"I'll come get it in the morning," Sandy said.

"Knock on the door, and I'll give you a cup of coffee."

Hugs all around. I was almost sorry to see them go. I wasn't looking forward to the scene with Andy.

I closed the door, and we stood for a moment in silence. Then we both started speaking at once.

When I realized that he was apologizing, too, I shut up.

"It was my fear coming out in anger," he explained. "When the dispatcher told me your message, I went crazy."

I, of course, began to cry, while he looked embarrassed.

"But, goddamn it, you shouldn't have gone to the park and put both of you in danger," he said.

He was right, but I was saved from admitting it by the telephone. A vaguely familiar woman's voice asked for Andy. He talked with his arm around me. It was obvious that he was being interviewed. He ran through the story in an extremely circumspect manner, using all the tortuous circumlocutions cops hold so dear, then handed the phone to me, with a wicked smile.

"Hello, Kate, it's Margaret Papadakis. I wonder if you would mind telling me about what happened in Withrow Park today. I gather you were quite the heroine."

It was the sound of someone speaking through clenched teeth.

CHAPTER

33

Andy left shortly after my conversation with Margaret, and didn't come back until 2:00, by which time I was long asleep. I woke just enough to notice he was there. He wriggled, settling himself into a comfortable position to sleep, rather like a dog circling his sleeping spot before he lies down. We were both too exhausted to do anything more than exchange affectionate murmurs.

The next morning we read all the papers over coffee. There were banner headlines in my own paper, with Margaret's story on the front page, along with statements from the publisher and managing editor. Both emphasized the presumption of innocence, and that Dickie had no criminal record. They had also provided him with a high-profile lawyer, the kind of guy who, when he takes a case, everyone assumes his client is guilty.

There were two more pages inside the front section devoted to the story. My eyewitness account was there, along with interviews with kids who were in the park when it happened, and predictable statements from some of my colleagues: "I can't believe it . . . he was so quiet . . . he just did his job . . . we never suspected . . . this can't be true." There was a photograph of Dickie and Beth, captioned, inevitably, "In happier days." And there was a picture of me, too.

"Margaret's story is a piece of work," Andy said, when it was his turn to read the story. "She doesn't seem to want you to get any credit in the arrest."

"And then the headline writers put 'Our Kate' all over the rest of the page," I laughed.

The *World* was low-key in its story. The self-important grey journal of record seldom stooped to reporting local stories, keeping its national audience in mind. Serial murder is still rare enough in this country that they did give it a full page, with a small story on the front. I was referred to as "a local sports reporter." So was Dickie.

The *Mirror* took Dickie's logo shot from his *Planet* column and blew it up to fill the tabloid front page, a nice touch in a competitive newspaper market. There were four more pages on Dickie and the arrest inside, but the scantily clad brunette on page three expressed no opinions.

Andy was out the door by 9:00, assuring me that any business the police had with me could be conducted over the phone. Personal business was another matter, but I didn't need to stay in the city. I called Jake and told him I would be able to make the Titan charter and packed for the six-day road trip to Detroit and Cleveland.

I was depressed, for some reason. I guess it was a natural rebound from the adrenalin high I'd been through the day before. I didn't much feel like a road trip, but staying home would be worse. I wanted to get away from the newspapers and broadcasts.

I got to the airport half an hour early, dropped off my bag with the travelling secretary, who gave me the gate number and my boarding pass, then went to the self-serve coffee shop to wait. Stinger Swain and Goober Grabowski were a few places ahead of me in line. They didn't see me, but I was close enough to overhear them.

"The way I figure it," Swain declaimed to his sidekick, "Preacher was just jealous. He wanted the little boy for his self."

Grabowski didn't share in his buddy's guffaws.

"I don't know, Stinger," he frowned. "The guy had a knife and all. I think it was pretty brave of Joe."

Wonder of wonder. Dissension in the redneck ranks.

"Don't you go getting soft on me," Swain scoffed, as they got to the cash register. "You got any of that funny money on you? I've only got American."

Grabowksi pulled out a handful of coloured Canadian bills and dropped a blue one on the counter.

"You're gonna owe me one in Dee-troit," he grumbled, picking up his change.

I couldn't resist stopping by their table.

"I see someone read the newspapers to you this morning, Stinger," I said.

"Oh, looky. Here's the lady detective," he sneered. "When you going to start wearing a badge?"

"Our heroine," Grabowski chimed in.

"I couldn't have done it without Preacher," I said. "He was the real hero. What he and his friend did really took balls. Don't you think?"

That shut them up. For the moment, anyway. I went to the farthest empty table I could find and opened my book.

Gradually, half a dozen other players drifted in to the coffee shop, dressed according to the Titan travel code, in jackets and ties. Some of them were more sartorially splendid than others. Eddie Carter had on his usual silk Italian number, with pleats in his pants straight out of the forties. Gloves was professorial in a tweed sportsjacket. Tiny challenged the seams of his pinstriped suit. Kid Cooper, the rookie, was with him, dressed in something that looked as if he had bought it for his high school graduation. He probably had. Atsuo Watanabe was a surprise, all in black and white, very high fashion, with an unconstructed jacket and soft kid leather shoes.

I overheard a lot more conversation about Dickie's arrest, of course. A couple of the players stopped by my table to talk about it. But Preacher didn't appear until just before it was time to board. When he walked into the departure lounge, Eddie Carter was the first to cross the room and shake his hand. He wasn't the only one.

It wasn't exactly high fives all around, but a dozen players offered manly punches on the shoulder and awkward pats on the back. Joe smiled shyly and mumbled his thanks.

We got on the plane and settled into our usual seats. First came Red O'Brien and the coaches and other team personnel, followed by the writers and broadcasters, with the players in their own territory in the rear. Joe ended up in the row just behind me, with Tiny on the aisle seat next to him.

"So, what do you think of the Preacher now, Kate Henry?" boomed the deposed first baseman. "Ain't he the man?"

"He sure is, Tiny," I said, over my shoulder. "How are you doing today, Joe?"

"I'm fine. How's T.C.?"

"I haven't seen him since last night, but I'm sure he's fine. He's going to be the most important kid in his class. He'll love it."

"Of course, it was just luck," Tiny said. "The man just happened to be at the right place. I can't remember when I've been invited over to Kate's house for some barbecue."

I turned in my seat to check that his teasing smile was in place before answering.

"If I had to feed you, Tiny, I'd have to take a second mortgage out on my house."

"And you know it," he said.

Keith Jarvis, the *Mirror* beat writer, was the last one on the plane, breathless and rumpled.

"Damn cab had a flat on the 427," he said, stepping over me to his window seat. His shoulder bag whacked me in the jaw. The plane's engines had started by the time he got his seat-belt fastened.

"You gotta get up a bit earlier in the morning, Keith," Tiny said. "Especially if you want to beat Kate Henry to a story."

Jarvis glared at me. I reached back and punched Tiny's knee.

"Well, Tiny," Jarvis said. "It's hard to compete with a paper that will do anything for a story, even hire a murderer."

I opened my book and got set for a bumpy ride.

CHAPTER

34

The sports sections of the Detroit papers featured stories about Joe's role in the capture of the Daylight Stalker, which gave the large crowd of reporters something extra to talk to him about before the game. I stood on the edge of the scrum outside the dugout and listened to the questions. It didn't take very long for them to get to the point.

"Was the man who disarmed the murderer your lover, Joe?"

The questioner was an overweight stringer for *USA Today.* Joe looked him in the eye and nodded.

"Yes, he was."

"Is he with you on the trip?"

"No. He has gone back to California. He has his own work to take care of."

"Do you think this will take some of the heat off you from the fans?"

"I haven't felt much heat from the fans," he said. "I didn't do what I did for the publicity. Or to take heat off, as you say. I'm just glad I was able to be of some help. Now, if you will excuse me, I have to get ready for the game."

The crowd dispersed when Joe left the dugout and went to the batting cage. One of the reporters came over to me. He is a man with whom I have had a sporadic relationship since I came on the beat. Sally calls him Mr. Same Time Next Year, since we only do it when I visit Detroit.

"So, you're right in the middle of the action again, Kate," he said. "Trouble seems to follow you around. Or do you go looking for it?"

"I do my best to avoid it," I said. "How was your winter?"

"I got married. How was yours?"

"Not as eventful as yours. Congratulations."

"That doesn't mean things have to change between us," he said.

"No, I suppose it doesn't," I said, wondering what I'd ever seen in the creep. "But I think I'll take a pass this time around."

"Suit yourself," he said, then walked away.

I sat on the bench and watched the Titans taking batting practice. They were laughing and playing the same tired jokes on each other they did every day. There's something comforting in the rituals, even for me. It seemed like just another night at the ballpark.

Until the fans arrived. Then it turned ugly. The rocket scientists in the bleachers didn't seem to have been impressed by Joe's heroics. The banners they hung in left field expressed their feelings eloquently: "Fairy go home," "Queer City," "The Pansy

Garden," and "Bugger off, Kelsey." When the Tiger left-fielder took his position, he went through an elaborate dumb-show of denial, and the banners were put away with glee until the bottom half of the inning.

Every time Joe came to bat, the chants started: "FAG-GOT, FAG-GOT." Whenever he went to left field, they threw things at him. He got drenched with beer several times. The umpires actually stopped the game at one point, when the barrage got really bad, and the stadium announcer told the fans that further behaviour of that sort would result in ejection and possible forfeiture of the game. Uniformed cops took up positions among the rowdier fans.

Joe ignored them, held himself in control, and turned his anger into his play. He hit a two-run home run and an RBI double. In the field, he made one spectacular diving catch of a ball that was destined for extra bases and jumped high at the fence to pull another ball back into the park. The final score was 3–2 for the Titans. It was all Joe's game, which made the fans even angrier.

In the clubhouse afterwards, the mood was chippy and defiant. Now Stinger and Goober were odd men out, as player after player praised Joe and condemned the fans. It was a tribal thing. When one of their own is under attack the way Joe was out there on that field, the members of the clan close ranks. Even Red O'Brien didn't temper his praise for his left-fielder.

"I've always said that this team can win the whole thing," Red said. "If Joe keeps playing the way he has been, he can win the whole thing by himself."

After I filed my story, I joined the other Toronto writers and the television crew in the bar for the usual post-game wind-down, and it was 3:00 in the morning by the time I got back to my room. Finally alone, I had to face what I had been avoiding since the afternoon before: remembering.

I began to shake and cry. I felt the fear I hadn't allowed myself to feel before. I thought about Dickie, about the sparks of remorse that had made him give himself away. And I thought about T.C., and what would have happened if we hadn't found him.

Then I thought about the other children and their shattered families. I finally fell asleep, the blankets wrapped around me like a shroud, and dreamed violence and rage.

In the morning, early, Andy phoned.

"I watched some of the game last night," he said. "That was pretty ugly."

"Yeah, but maybe it was the best thing that could have happened," I said, then told him about the players' reactions. "I expect that it will put a lot of people on Joe's side. What's happening up there? Has Dickie confessed?"

"He says he's waiting for the best offer from the papers. He's asked for a lap-top computer to write his memoirs."

"Jesus."

"Typical. We don't need a confession, though. We've searched his house and found enough evidence to tie him to the three murders here and the ones in Timmins."

"What sort of evidence?" I asked, not sure I really wanted to know.

"Newspaper clippings in scrapbooks, some Polaroids. He had a locked filing cabinet in his den. His wife was forbidden to go into the room."

"How is she?"

"Not great. There are reporters and cameras camped on her front lawn. Her parents have flown in from Vancouver to be with her, and I imagine she'll go back with them as soon as we're through with her."

"Didn't she suspect anything?"

"No, and she's beating herself up about it. She sees things in retrospect that she didn't at the time and blames herself for the deaths."

"Poor kid."

"Yeah."

"How do you feel?"

"The way I always do after a case. Relieved. Depressed. Sorry I couldn't have stopped him sooner."

"And angry?"

"A little bit. I wish you were here."

"So do I."

"I'm sorry about the way it has been for the last little while."

"So am I."

"It won't get better, you know. I'm a cop. That comes first."

"I know."

"How do you feel about that?"

"I don't know."

"You're gone for a week?"

"Yeah. We go to New York after the game tomorrow night."

"I'll call you there."

"If you like." I wasn't giving him much. There was a bit of a silence.

"I'll look in on T.C. and Sally, make sure they're all right. And Elwy."

"That would be nice." More silence.

"Oh, by the way. The department wants to give you another citation. Also Joe and Sandy."

"Oh, goody."

"Damn it, Kate. Stop doing that. I can't stand noncommittal. Yell at me, why don't you?"

"I'm not mad, just confused. I'm delighted about the citation, especially for Sandy and Joe. A little macho recognition will go good right about now."

"Knowing me hasn't been very safe for you."

"It's not your fault that I keep sticking my nose in. I'm sorry I'm being like this, but I'm just emotionally exhausted. And physically, too, for that matter."

"Well, get back to sleep. I'll call you again."

"If you like."

I went back to sleep, an escape from things I didn't want to deal with. Or couldn't. My last waking thought was a belated pang of anguish for poor Beth Greaves and her baby son.

At 2:00 in the afternoon, the phone woke me again. The housekeeper wanted me to take down my Do Not Disturb sign so her staff could clean the room. I told them to come on in and went down for some lunch, stopping at the newsstand on the way.

Happily, columns in both the major newspapers condemned the behaviour of the fans. Their boorishness had created the backlash I had hoped for. Maybe things would ease up for Joe after all.

After lunch, I went back to my room and worked out, using the back of a chair for my barre, sweating off my blues. I took a long shower, then went down to the lobby to wait for the ballpark bus. The autograph hounds swarmed any player who let himself be caught. Watanabe smiled at me from the middle of one pack. I waved.

Life goes on. Baseball goes on too, no matter what happens in the real world. The teams are in a cocoon of schedules, routines, game times, bus times. Their only contact with the outside world is through the adoring fans, and that's not reality either.

The bus pulled in at 4:45. The players piled on discussing that day's episode on *The Young and The Restless*. Stinger yelled at the bus driver. Tiny began teasing. Hugh Marsh, head down, worked with his stats. I opened my book.

The sun was shining. It was a great day for a ball game.